CW00348511

A Brooke and Daniel Psychological Thriller

DEVIANCE

J.F.PENN

This book is a work of fiction. The characters, incidents and dialogue
are drawn from the author's imagination and are not to be construed
as real. Any resemblance to actual events or persons, living or dead, is
fictionalized or coincidental.

Deviance
Copyright © J.F. Penn (2015). All rights reserved.

www.JFPenn.com

ISBN: 978-1-913321-29-1

The right of Joanna Penn to be identified as the author of this work has
been asserted by the author in accordance with the Copyright, Designs
and Patents Act,1988. All rights reserved. No part of this publication may
be reproduced, stored in a retrieval system, or transmitted, in any form,
or by any means, electronic, mechanical, photocopying, recording or
otherwise, without the prior permission of the publishers.

This book is sold subject to the condition that it shall not,
by way of trade or otherwise, be lent, resold, hired out, or otherwise
circulated without the author's prior consent in any form of binding
or cover other than that in which it is published and without a similar
condition being imposed on the subsequent purchaser.

Requests to publish work from this book should be sent to:
joanna@CurlUpPress.com

Cover and Interior Design: JD Smith Design

Printed by Lightning Source Ltd

www.CurlUpPress.com

"Do not conform to the pattern of this world ..."
Romans 12:2

"You were wild once. Don't let them tame you."
Isadora Duncan

CHAPTER 1

THE TRAIN RATTLED ALONG the tracks on the brick bridge above their heads, lending a rhythm to the words spoken below. London was never completely dark, the city lights lit up the sky at all hours, but tonight it seemed that the darkness was deeper, the space between the stars an all-consuming black. As the nearby church bells tolled midnight, the small group gathered together. Candles flickered, casting a halo around their heads, bent in respect to those lost here.

They stood in front of a pair of tall gates, closed and locked to segregate this small area of scrubland in the heart of Southwark, a stone's throw from the river and affluent Borough Market, at the junction between Redcross Way and Union Street. The dull metal struts of the gates were alive with multi-colored ribbons, each inscribed with a name. They represented those whose remains lay under the earth of Cross Bones Graveyard, names gathered from records of history in an attempt to personalize the dead. Their shades walk these streets still, a sliver of their memory in the hip-swinging walk of sex workers, their song in the local pubs, their laughter in the late-night bar crawlers.

"I was born a goose of Southwark by the grace of Mary Overie, whose Bishop gives me license to sin within the Liberty."

The words of local poet John Constable rang out in the night air, his poem a tribute to the women who had once plied their trade here under the authority of the medieval church. They were known as Winchester Geese, controlled by the Bishop of Winchester and their taxes filled the coffers of the church. But in death, these women and their bastard children were outcasts, denied a burial in consecrated ground. Tonight these Outcast Dead would be honored in the memories of those who walked in their footsteps centuries later.

A young man with a guitar played a mournful dirge, his voice clear in the night air. His blond hair reflected the light from the candles, a blue streak through it giving him a rakish look. Jamie Brooke stood on the edge of the group listening to his song. She held a candle in both hands and gazed into the flame as her thoughts shifted to the memory of her own daughter, Polly, who had died six months ago from a terminal illness. The ache of grief still made her breath catch on days when her guard was down, but here, amongst these other mourners, the memory was tender.

A smile played across her lips. Polly would have loved this group of colorful people who lived outside the conformity of the city suits. These were no mourners in dull black. There were several women from the Prostitutes' Collective, holding a banner high. They honored their sisters and brothers who had died servicing society, courted and loved in secret while rejected and hated in public. One woman wore a belt of a skirt, tall spike heels revealing killer legs. Jamie caught the woman's face in profile, realizing that it was a man in drag, or perhaps someone transgender. Not that it mattered here, in the city where all could find a place.

As the group joined together in song, Jamie recognized a woman in the crowd, her pixie-cropped ash-blonde hair shining almost white in the candlelight. Known to Jamie only as O, she wore light makeup, her petite features making her look like a teenager, wrapped tight in a black denim jacket and skinny jeans. But Jamie knew what lay beneath her clothes. She remembered her first glimpse of O, dancing naked at the Torture Garden nightclub, her full-body octopus tattoo undulating as she moved. She was certainly no teenager.

A woman started crying silently and O put her arms around her, solidarity clear in the gesture. Jamie noticed other signs of a tight-knit community as people held hands, love evident in the way they looked at each other. For a moment, Jamie wished she had that kind of community. But her years as a police officer and caretaker of her sick daughter had meant little time for friends.

What would my ex-colleagues think of this gathering? Jamie thought. This patchwork of personalities held together by respect for the dead and perhaps, by a hope that they could transcend the bleak future of those gone before. Jamie knew that many here would go out tonight and trade their bodies for money in the hotels and backstreets of Southwark. It ever was and ever will be. She looked up at the stars, which had witnessed lust in these streets since Roman times. Human nature didn't change. There would always be sex and death, drinking and drugs, peace and war, violence and love. There would always be light in the dark too, and Jamie hoped to be one of the bright ones in this borough.

"Tonight we march along the same streets as the Outcast Dead, in memory of those who came before us and the sisters and brothers we have lost along the way."

The strident voice echoed through the street, an Irish lilt evident in her tone. It belonged to the leader of the event and one of the personalities of Southwark: Magda Raven. That's what she called herself anyway – no one seemed to know her real name. She was tall, built like a pro netball player, her long limbs muscled and toned. She wore a tight black t-shirt and black jeans, both arms displaying full-sleeve tattoos that covered them from shoulder to wrist.

One arm was tattooed like a stained glass window, with the figure of Mary Magdalene kneeling in front of Christ in the garden of Gethsemane. The other arm was a riot of ravens, wings beating in a tornado of wind and nature, as if they would lift from her skin. Jamie had heard Magda called an urban shaman, that she walked the city with a vision of the other worlds it contained, and she had heard of Magda's campaign to turn the graveyard into a memorial park. The woman was seemingly unstoppable, a hero to the local people and a thorn in the side of developers who wanted to make a tidy profit from this valuable land.

The cemetery had been so full of human remains in the late nineteenth century that it was closed as a health hazard and became an urban myth over time, a legendary graveyard for the forgotten dead. Thousands were buried here, and the land remained locked in dispute.

"Let us honor their memory now by tying ribbons in their name."

Magda's last few words were drowned out by the rising sound of a hymn and feet stamping to a rousing chorus.

A group of people rounded the corner at the end of the street. They were mostly middle-aged, more women than men, their voices strident as they sang. They carried banners embroidered with scenes of pastoral perfection and emblazoned with slogans. *No sin in Southwark. Hate the sin, love the sinner.* At the bottom of the banners, their allegiance was printed in black: *The Society for the Suppression of Vice.*

Magda pointedly ignored the singing and continued with the service, indicating that those present should come forward and tie new ribbons to the gates next to the faded ones from previous months. O walked forward, kissing a pink ribbon before tying it to the gate, her head bent in remembrance.

"Dirty fucking whores."

The shout came from behind the Society for the Suppression of Vice, and some of the singers turned, faces

4

shocked by the language. But others glared at the group gathered by the gates, supportive of the words that condemned those they considered unclean. Emboldened by the harsh words, the Society singers took a step forward as if to push back the people who offended them with their mere existence.

They filled the width of the street, their dark coats and muted colors a dull contrast to the bright clothes of the sex workers and their supporters. Jamie noticed that some of the girls pulled hoods up, shielding their faces in fear of recognition.

Magda Raven stood silent for a moment, looking towards the Society group with fire in her eyes. She attached her own ribbon to the gate and lifted a candle towards the sky.

"Mother Goddess, virgin and whore, from whom all life comes."

A low hiss came from the Society at her words, and they took another step towards the group.

"May we who remember the Outcast Dead be blessed on this night and protected on the nights to come."

Magda poured some of the wax from her candle onto the bottom of the gates, marking it in remembrance. Then she walked through the crowd and began to lead the sex workers along the street, down Redcross Way towards the river. The Society walked behind, matching their steps.

Jamie lingered towards the back of the group alongside some of the male sex workers and local campaigners. Her senses were alert to the possible threat here, honed by years in the police. Most of those who marched under the banners of the Society were harmless middle-aged women from Southwark Cathedral who thought they were doing good by denouncing sin on the streets. Their eyes were guarded, their fingers gripped their banners tightly, armor against being polluted by the sin of the fallen.

But Jamie saw hate and fanaticism in the eyes of some of

them. She had seen that same look in the eyes of racist thugs, religious fanatics and, once, in the smoky Hellfire Caves of West Wycombe, where she had almost died.

At the end of Redcross Way, Magda led the group into Park Street and then Stoney Street. The bars of Borough had mostly closed, but there were still a few people in the streets, laughing as they headed home. Some noticed the two disparate groups, the calm slow steps of the colorful sex workers, followed by the tramp of the Society.

"Come 'ere, darlin'," a man shouted across the road at one of the younger girls. "I've got somethin' that'll put a smile on yer face ... or *somethin'* on your face at least." He guffawed and his mates collapsed in laughter as they staggered off down the road.

O took the hand of the younger woman and they kept walking, faces set in respect, some looking down at the candles they held. Jamie knew that they must hear such words often. It came with the job, but that didn't make it right.

The group approached the end of Stoney Street near the medieval Clink prison, where old warehouses had been turned into luxury apartments overlooking the Thames. Magda turned right, leading the group towards the ruins of Winchester Palace. The monthly vigil always culminated at Southwark Cathedral just a little further on, where they would leave a symbolic wreath in memory of the unconsecrated dead.

The great rose window atop a high stone wall was the only thing that remained of the original twelfth-century palace, illuminated by spotlights at night. This was where the Bishops of Winchester had lived until the seventeenth century, rich men who often held the post as Chancellor. The coffers of the church in this, the Liberty, were filled from the proceeds of the stews, the brothels, the Clink prison, gaming, theatres and all manner of pleasures suppressed in the City across the river. This was where London used to sin – and where, perhaps, it still did. Jamie remained at the back of the group, a buffer between the working girls and the protestors. She felt the eyes of the Society members on her back as she walked, and she wondered briefly what they thought of her.

As the first of the group passed into the light of the Winchester Palace ruins, a scream rang out, a long shrill note that pierced the night.

CHAPTER 2

JAMIE STARTED FORWARD, HER body instinctively reacting from her police training, her pulse racing with adrenalin. Her eyes scanned the scene. There was no obvious danger.

"Stay back," Magda's strong voice called out. "Move away now."

Jamie pushed through the throng even as the group surged forward to look. Human nature was ever to gaze at whatever horror lay beyond. Some of them pulled out their phones to take pictures.

She reached the edge of the railing that protected the ruined foundations and looked down. In the middle of the courtyard, a man lay spread-eagle on his back. Jamie automatically processed the crime scene in her mind, as she had always done in the police, scanning the area and noting the details of the body. The man's arms were a ruin of bloody flesh, the skin flayed off with a very sharp knife by the look of the clean wound edges. He wore the remains of a shredded cassock, slashed around the torso, the white collar still visible. His mouth was stuffed with white feathers and more lay around him, stained by his own blood.

"Call the police," Jamie shouted, her tone authoritative. "We need to secure the scene."

As Magda pulled her phone out, Jamie ran down the steps towards the man. The blood around him was fresh and he could still be alive. Stepping carefully so as not to disturb the area too much, Jamie bent to feel the pulse at his neck. There was nothing, but there still might be hope. She had to try.

With the cuff of her sleeve over her fingers, she tugged the feathers from his mouth, the goose down stuffed so deep into his throat that she couldn't get them all out.

After a moment, Jamie stopped. There was no way this man was alive. His face was frozen in agony, his eyes bulging and bloodshot. His thick dark hair was shot through with a streak of white. Jamie was aware of the lack of life in him. His body was still warm but the essence of it had gone, leaving only this ruined flesh. It was now more important to preserve the scene for those who could look into his death and bring him some kind of justice.

Jamie wiped away the prick of tears, frustration at another wasted life and the fact that she would not be on the police team that would investigate his murder. Her statement would be taken, as she had once taken them, but she would be on the outside this time.

Who was this man and why was his body left here? Was it a statement to the community and, if so, which part?

Jamie looked up at the faces staring down at her. At one end, the frightened faces of the sex workers and at the other, the hard expressions of the Society for the Suppression of Vice. Sirens rang out in the London night as the police arrived on the scene.

***

Dale Cameron stood in the shadows of Winchester Square, his heart pounding as the rush flooded through him. The sense of almost being discovered gave him an added thrill. He knew he should leave but he couldn't bring himself to move just yet. The initial scream of panic at discovery of the body had given way to a low hubbub. He could hear someone weeping. He breathed deeply and let the sounds sink into his consciousness as he savored the aftermath of violence.

He clutched a dark blue waterproof bag in his fist. It was designed to keep things dry while kayaking on the river, perfect for the collection of his trophies. It was heavy now, weighed down by the bloody skin inside. He stroked the outside of the bag with tentative fingers. The kill was nothing compared to the harvest of his bloody keepsakes.

Sirens burst through the noise of the disturbed crowd. Dale snapped out of his reverie. The sound belonged to his other self, his daytime self, and his phone would soon be ringing with the news.

A slow smile crept across his face.

As a Detective Superintendent he could even stay and help process the crime scene. The officers on duty would respect him even more for doing grunt work far below his station. Part of him was tempted by the idea – part of him wanted to skate so close to the edge that they might even suspect him. But no … He shook his head. There was too much at stake now and he was so close to his goal. These small purges were nothing to what he had planned for Southwark. For now, he needed to get away from the scene before it was locked down.

Dale walked through the back streets of London Bridge to his car with a confident stride. Not too slow, not too fast. Nothing that would draw attention to himself. He placed the bag in the trunk and got into the driver's seat, giving himself a moment before completing the final phase of his ritual.

He leaned over and opened the glove compartment, then reached in and pulled out a pot of Ponds Cold Cream. He unscrewed the top and lifted it to his nose, closing his eyes as he inhaled the floral scent.

Dale smiled. His mother had had such beautiful skin, with the translucence of Egyptian alabaster. He used to watch her as a boy as she smoothed cream into her arms and hands, massaging it slowly until it had all disappeared, leaving only a trace of scent in the air. One day, she had turned to him, the sunlight from the window a halo around her golden hair. *Come here, darling. Let me put some on you.* He had stood between her knees as she took a dab from the fragrant jar. The lotion was slick on her palms as she rubbed it between them and then she took his arm and touched him with cool fingers. Goosebumps rippled over Dale's skin at the memory, the sensation clear in his mind, a moment of happiness. But then … his face darkened and he screwed the top back on the cream, slamming it back into the glove compartment. He would not sully the perfect memory tonight.

CHAPTER 3

HIGH CEILINGS OF PANELED glass supported by the green pillars of Borough Market allowed the light to flood into even the inner corners of the building. There had been a food market here since the eleventh century, but these days it was aimed more at the high-end restaurants and well-paid foodies of the city. Jamie walked past an artisan baker, who piled sourdough and spelt loaves next to tempting sticky fudge brownies. She inhaled the smell of fresh bread and baked sugar goodies, sweetness lingering on the back of her throat. Her stomach rumbled in anticipation, but the problem with Borough was the sheer volume of choice. It was hard to know what to choose when every stall contained another tiny world of culinary pleasure.

Jamie was exhausted from last night. The police had arrived quickly and taken statements from those people who remained, although many had vanished into the darkness when the body had been discovered. Because of her history and contacts, her own statement had been processed quickly. She had been able to leave before the others, but she couldn't get the image of the man's face out of her mind and sleep had been hard to come by.

She weaved her way through the market, navigating the early shoppers, glancing at the abundance of produce as she passed. One stall was covered with baskets of mushrooms:

wild, golden chanterelles and purplish pied bleu lying next to the thick trunks of king oysters. There were butchers with fresh game, carcasses of ducks and deer hanging down outside the shops where men with heavy hands served packets of paper-wrapped choice cuts. Proud chefs sold specialized wares – cider from a local orchard, honey made from urban Hackney bees, cured prosciutto from the happiest free-range, acorn-fed pigs. There was also a row of street-food stalls and coffee carts at the back near Southwark Cathedral, and Jamie wound her way through the crowds in that direction.

She was beginning to find her way around after moving into Southwark last month. Her old flat in Lambeth had become unbearable after Polly's death, memories slamming into her whenever she walked in the door. Jamie had wept in the empty room before locking it for the last time, but her daughter was free now and Jamie needed to live as Polly had asked her to. She had handed over all her old cases after resigning from the Metropolitan Police, and closed that door as well. But she couldn't bring herself to leave London. The city held her tightly, curled itself within her.

Jamie caught sight of Detective Sergeant Alan Missinghall at the edge of the throng, his six-foot-five frame dwarfing the people around him. He was struggling to hold two coffee cups along with several bags brimming with pastries. Jamie grinned as she hurried through the crowds towards him, happy that some things never changed. Missinghall always made food a priority.

"Let me help with that," she said. He turned at her approach.

"Hi, Jamie. Good to see you."

Missinghall handed her the pastries and bent to kiss her cheek. Jamie was slightly bemused by the affection, something he would never have shown on the job. They had worked together on a number of cases and he had been junior to her at the time, as a Detective Constable. He had covered her back during a couple of dangerous investigations and was probably her closest friend in the Met by the end.

"Let's go sit in the churchyard with these," she said, leading the way through the gates and into the grounds of Southwark Cathedral, where they found a free bench in a patch of sun. They sat in comfortable silence for a moment sipping coffee as the busy market bustled behind them and the calls of the market traders echoed across the little square.

"How's business then?" Missinghall asked, as he started into the second cheese and ham croissant. He leaned forward, making sure the crumbs fell to the pavement below. Pigeons came pecking within seconds and cleared up his scraps. This area was teeming with bird life, drawn by the rich pickings from Borough Market.

"It's quite a different side of the city, that's for sure." Jamie smiled. "But it's interesting work so far, especially round here. I got a few clients within days of putting up the new website. Thanks for putting the word out."

Missinghall grinned. "Recommending you is good for my reputation. You're quite the celebrity, to be honest. And that pic on the website is a hit."

Jamie blushed a little. She had used a picture of herself in black leather, standing with arms crossed against her motorbike, black hair loose in the wind and the City of London in the background. Her gaze was no-nonsense and capable, with a hint of challenge. It was a look she had never been able to fully embrace when she worked as a Detective Sergeant, but now she worked as a private investigator, she could do whatever she liked.

It was hardly idyllic, however, and Jamie pushed down her guilt at lying to Missinghall. Her new business as a private investigator was only just paying the bills, and the cases were dull and repetitive. Prenuptial investigations and matrimonial surveillance were not quite as fascinating as homicide cases. It seemed that the pull of death was in her blood, echoing the pulse of the city. She missed the all-consuming cases in the way that an addict missed a fix – with the sure knowledge that it was killing as she indulged. She missed the camaraderie and the sense of doing something good for the community – though she didn't miss the paperwork, or Detective Superintendent Dale Cameron.

"And what about you, Al?" Jamie said. "How's life as a DS?"

"The promotion's alright and the missus appreciates it. But to be honest, I miss the way we worked together. I guess I'll get used to it soon enough. Nothing stays the same in this city ..." Missinghall's voice trailed off as he looked up at the Gothic cathedral in front of him. "Well, nothing except the architecture anyway. I'm glad we can still meet up though, and you know I'm happy to help out if I can."

Jamie took another sip of coffee, letting the hot, bitter liquid soothe her tired brain.

"Do you know anything about the homicide that happened here last night?"

Missinghall chuckled. "I thought you'd want to know more about it when I saw your name on the witness statements. We off the record?"

"Of course. I'm part of the community here now and I was there, so ..."

Missinghall nodded.

"Turns out that the murdered man, Nicholas Randolph, worked here at Southwark Cathedral. He was part of the community outreach team, working closely with the toms. There have been suggestions that he used to be a sex worker himself, but not confirmed as yet. You might be able to find that out more easily than we can. People round here are pretty tight-lipped about that kind of thing."

Jamie frowned. "What about his arms? They looked flayed."

"We got some pictures from the next of kin. Randolph had full-sleeve tattoos that revealed quite a bit about his past. A combination of religious iconography and gay-pride images."

Jamie raised an eyebrow. "You can see how some might have objected to that. Any suspects?"

Missinghall shook his head slowly. "You know I can't talk about that." He paused and looked up at the sky. He took a deep breath and Jamie waited, taking another sip of coffee and allowing him the silence.

Finally, his dark eyes met hers and she saw concern there. "Look, tell your mates round here to keep an eye out." He paused. "Off the record, this isn't the first homicide with this MO. There've been two other bodies found recently in Southwark – undesirable characters by some definitions. They also had flayed parts of their bodies where tattoos had been excised. But they were illegal immigrants and this is the first high-profile case. A man of the church, whatever his past. Even the Mayor has gotten involved. With the run-up to the election, he'll be antsy to get this solved."

"Is Dale Cameron really running?" Jamie asked.

Missinghall grimaced at the name. Dale Cameron was a rising star in the Met with the looks of a corporate CEO and the slippery shoulders to match. He had been their superior officer on previous cases, and crossing him had directly led to Jamie's resignation from the police. When she'd woken from nightmares of smoke and burning body parts, she'd been sure that he had been in the drug-fueled haze of the Hellfire Caves.

"Yes," Missinghall said, shaking his head. "He's got a good chance, as well. Loads of the top brass want someone with a hard line on crime in the Mayor's seat. And Cameron is a hard bastard, that's for sure." He sighed. "But whatever we think of him, he certainly gets results. Crime's down across the city. He's cracking down on immigrants and he's moving the homeless and mentally ill out of the central areas."

"That's what people want, I guess," Jamie said. "As long as it doesn't upset their own lives in any way."

Missinghall looked at his watch. "I've gotta go, sorry." He stood up and brushed pastry crumbs from his suit. "Do this again sometime?"

Jamie smiled up at him. "That would be great. Thanks for coming, Al. Stay in touch."

Missinghall turned and walked away but after a few steps he came back, his eyes serious.

"There's also been a rise in reported missing persons around here," he said. "Prostitutes, illegal immigrants, homeless addicts. You know we don't have the resources to pursue all the cases in detail, especially with people who move on so quickly. But it's worrying, so stay out of trouble, Jamie."

Jamie put her hand on her heart and gave him a look that made him grin before he walked off into the crowded streets. But she knew she couldn't let it go. The police would do their investigation into the murder, but there was something wrong in Southwark and after last night, she was already involved

Jamie stood and walked to the cathedral door, her eyes drawn to the flint cobbles embedded in the walls on either side. She reached out to stroke one of the rocks, its surface smooth and almost metallic to the touch, the colors layered like the center of the earth. Then she pushed open the door to Southwark Cathedral and walked inside, determined to find something of Nicholas Randolph here.

The Gothic cathedral was a mixture of the architecture of ancient faith and a modern sensibility, appealing to tourists and the faithful alike. A series of medieval bosses were attached to the back wall, fastened there as remnants of the fifteenth-century church. One of them portrayed the Devil devouring Judas, its face blackened by fire and time.

One of the stone tombs caught Jamie's eye. It had *Thomas Cure 1588* written above it, a memorial for a saddler to the Tudor King Edward VI, Queen Mary and Queen Elizabeth. With a prominent ribcage and skeletal bones with an over-large head, it looked nothing like the tombs usually seen in churches. Instead of a representation of the man in life, this was a cadaver effigy, a decomposing body, a direct *memento mori* to remind people that our physical remains will soon be as this. Jamie shivered a little in the cold of the stone church.

"May I help you?"

Jamie turned to find a bright-eyed older woman, leaflets clutched in her hand and a 'Volunteer' badge pinned neatly to her lilac knitted sweater. Jamie smiled.

"Thank you, that would be great. I'm doing some research about the area and I've heard that the medieval church here was involved with the brothels. Is that true?"

The woman frowned, her face showing distaste. "As much as many of us would like to erase the past, it's the truth. The church used to be St Mary Overie and it was owned by the Bishop of Winchester. He licensed the stews, as they were known, in Southwark for four hundred years. But of course, that was a long time ago and we are now actively working to clean up the community, to rid it of that dirty past."

"I'm interested in the work the church does with the community," Jamie said. "Is there someone in particular I could talk to about that?"

The woman smiled, clearly relieved to be focusing on a more suitable topic. "Well, we're all involved," she said, pride evident in her voice. "Was there anything in particular you wanted to find out about? Volunteering perhaps …" She looked Jamie up and down, in the way only an older woman could. "We have rehab groups, too."

At her words, Jamie became more aware of her appearance. She'd lost weight recently, eating only for fuel these days. Her cheekbones stood out against pale skin. She rarely wore makeup and she tied her dyed black hair into a tight bun most days. But drug-addict chic was not really the professional look she was aiming for.

"Did you know Nicholas Randolph?" Jamie asked.

The woman froze, her breath catching at the name. She put a hand against the wall, her head drooping a little. Tears glistened in her eyes.

"I'm sorry," Jamie whispered. "Were you close?"

"He was Nick to us," the woman said. "And he was a good man, despite what some said about his past." A hard edge came into her voice at that. "But the Lord forgives and washes our sins whiter than snow. The darker spark within us may lapse into old habits but even that can be forgiven. Repentance is a daily practice after all, and I'm afraid that Southwark more than most is testament to the dual nature of sinner and saint. Nick was both, as are we all."

"Was his community outreach program supported by all in the church?"

The woman hesitated and doubt flickered in her eyes. "Yes, of course, we're an inclusive church. We have an altar for the victims of AIDS ... Although, of course we cannot ignore what the Bible says about sexual sin. Nick was more tolerant than many, for sure, and he worked with some ..." She paused and shook her head. "Well, let's just say that I'm not sure there's anyone who can replace Nick in that particular part of the community outreach program." The woman shuffled her leaflets and then handed one to Jamie. "Here's some information about the church windows and the main tombs of interest. I'll leave you to continue alone."

The woman turned away to greet a family of American tourists who would be unlikely to ask such difficult questions.

Jamie walked towards the middle of the church and

paused in front of a stained glass window portraying characters from Shakespeare's plays. This had been the playwright's borough, back when theatre was part of the pleasure bank of the Thames alongside the prostitutes, bear baiting and gambling dens. The replica of the Globe Theatre stood a few streets away, and the stained glass honored the greatest of the Bard's plays. Prospero commanded the tempest with Caliban at his feet, Hamlet stood contemplating the skull of Horatio and the donkey-headed Bottom cavorted with pixies, while around them, all the world continued to be a stage.

At the very back corner of the cathedral, Jamie found the chapel to the victims of AIDS. A young man knelt on an altar cushion, his eyes closed, lips moving in silent prayer. There was a noticeboard set up by the side and Jamie walked closer to see what the church was involved in.

There were pictures from community events, people smiling at sausage-sizzles under rain-soaked skies, children making origami animals to accompany Noah into the ark. In one picture, Jamie spotted Nicholas Randolph, his dark hair recognizable with the streak of white. He looked younger in life, his face relaxed and happy. He wore a shirt with sleeves rolled up, revealing a rainbow on one arm, the promise from God not to destroy the world again and now a symbol for acceptance. Next to him, her face alive with laughter, was Magda Raven.

CHAPTER 4

Blake Daniel tried to concentrate on the document on his screen. He willed his brain to conjure the next sentence and strained against the need to get up. He swallowed and clenched his fists under the desk.

Just one drink and the anxiety would subside.

This need for alcohol was a permanent thudding in his blood. His father's recent death and the discovery of a dark family history had sent him back into the tangled embrace of the tequila bottle. But now he was determined to pull away. Jamie managed her grief at the loss of her daughter and she was much harder hit than he was. Coffee would be a better remedy – at least for now.

Avoiding the critical eye of his ever-watchful manager, Margaret, Blake walked upstairs, out of the research area of the British Museum into the Great Court. It was a stunning marble courtyard with glass panels overhead that allowed the sun to touch every corner, a magnificent setting for the treasures within. Blake loved his job as an artifact researcher at the museum and every time he walked these halls, he marveled again at how lucky he was to work here.

He grabbed a coffee and a cupcake from the posh bakery in the forecourt, then found a place to sit so he could look out at the crowd. He popped a couple of headache pills and then sat for a moment, watching the people go by. He tried to guess the nationalities of those who walked past, a game he often played here in the city where all could find a place. Blake felt at home in London, where his own mixed-race heritage was a cultural norm. His mother was Nigerian, his father Swedish, and his caramel skin and blue eyes were less unusual here than in either of their native countries. Not that he had been to either. He listened to chattering voices around him, most in languages he couldn't even guess at, let alone understand. Perhaps it was time to visit.

Blake sipped his coffee, holding the hot brew between gloved hands. The thin leather hid deep scars across his skin from years of abuse. His father had tried to beat the Devil from his son, intending to destroy the ability to read objects and see visions from the past, or even another realm. But the beatings hadn't worked and the visions still came – sometimes as a gift and sometimes a curse. Blake had reconciled himself to his scars years ago, but now he was almost glad of them, a physical reminder that his father had even existed at all. After years of hating the man, his death hadn't brought peace, only more questions.

A gaggle of chattering schoolchildren caught Blake's eye, their laughter a welcome remedy to his melancholy. As they walked past, the shifting crowd around them parted for a second and Blake saw someone in their midst, a craggy face with a hint of familiarity. The man's eyes were a piercing blue, his features sculpted by northern winds, a scar across his nose like a mountain gulley. His body was like a menhir carved from ancient rock. He was still, his limbs tense. It was as if he waited for something – or someone.

Blake shivered, his skin goosebumps as he remembered the vision of the bloody rite of Odin, a human sacrifice to the gods of the north that he had glimpsed through the Galdrabók, a grimoire of Icelandic spells. His father had kept the powerful book under lock and key, but now it lay wrapped in sailcloth under Blake's own bed. He sometimes looked at the runes within, his gloved fingers tracing the angular lines that marked out his name as gifted, wondering about the others whose names were etched in a similar fashion. For the men who renewed the sacrifice of Ymir were his kin, and he saw an echo of them in the man here now.

He stood, trying to see the man more clearly even as the tourists whirled about, sweeping him out of view. Blake walked quickly towards the place the man had been standing, but he was gone. If he had even been there. Blake rubbed his forehead, urging the pain to subside. Could his visions be bleeding over into the real world? Or was he just seeing his father's face in the visage of another old man?

Blake walked back to the research area and pushed the glimpse of the man from his mind. His supervisor, Margaret, gave him a stern look, as she always did when he took too many breaks for her workaholic sensibility. She beckoned him into her small office.

Time to go on the offensive, Blake thought. He smiled, meeting Margaret's eyes with a direct gaze that made most women blush, a hint of promise for pleasures after dark. He had the look of a boy-band singer after a night partying, perennial stubble and close-cropped dark hair, and Blake knew he could turn on the charm when needed. He walked into Margaret's office, a mischievous smile on his lips.

"I've had some ideas about what we could call this new exhibition," he said, seating himself on the side of her desk, leaning towards her a little, his posture deliberately relaxed.

Margaret was the archetype of a middle-aged museum researcher, a little wide in the hips, no makeup, greying hair. But Blake liked that in an academic. One of his idols was Mary Beard, a professor of classics at Cambridge who brought Roman culture to life with her down-to-earth ways, uncaring of what the world thought of her looks while she stunned the public with her brilliant mind.

"You know that's up to the marketing team," Margaret said. "They're trying their best with the – unusual – material."

"How about the Las Vegas of Londonium," Blake said with a cheeky smile. He indicated the clay sculpture of a phallus lying on Margaret's desk. "Or Cocks of the Capital."

Margaret's mouth twitched.

"Cock of Ages?" Blake added.

She couldn't help but laugh at that. The musical, *Rock of Ages*, played down the road from the museum and was popular with tourists.

"Hmm, not sure that will fly," she said. "Although it looks like we're going to have to make it over-eighteens only."

"Better for marketing anyway," Blake said. "After all, the British Museum does have one of the largest collection of pornography in the world. Bless those Victorians."

Few were aware that the British Museum had the Secretum, founded in 1865 after the Obscene Publications Act, which preserved a chronology of pornography from the era. Blake stood up to leave.

"Can you shut the door a minute?" Margaret said, her voice suddenly serious. Blake pushed it shut, and the click of the door echoed in the pit of his stomach.

He sat back down on the chair opposite her.

"How's your paper coming along?" she asked, her voice losing all trace of flirtation now. "You seem to be behind … again."

Blake looked away. "I know. I'm sorry – my father's death …"

"I'm sorry about his passing, but we have a hard deadline on this exhibition. You know that. I need researchers who can deliver on time, and you've been repeatedly absent or late this last year." She paused. "Sometimes when you come in, I know you've been drinking, Blake." She pulled a paper from a folder next to her computer. "This is a formal warning about your behavior. It goes on your record and it means you're on notice."

Blake took the paper, but he couldn't read the words. They swam in front of his eyes, a mixture of legalistic terminology and HR gobbledygook. If only he could just have a drink. It would help his concentration.

At heart, he knew the discipline was deserved but it felt like he'd been slammed into a wall. His life was a balancing act, for sure, but he had thought he was managing it well enough. This job was stability even as his personal life was in shambles. He couldn't lose it.

"Blake, do you understand what this means?" Margaret's voice was a little softer now.

He nodded.

"Yes, I … I need to get back to work." He waved the paper, attempting a smile. "Lots to do."

Margaret nodded. "I'll expect an update at the end of the week."

Blake left Margaret's office and went back to his own desk, a little corner haven in the bustle of the museum. He sat down heavily and stared at his computer screen for a moment. He ran his gloved fingers along the edge of the desk, considering the possibility of just walking out.

The craving for a drink was overwhelming, but he had removed the flask of vodka from his bottom drawer last week in one of his attempts to go cold turkey.

There was a bar across the street, though.

He only had to walk upstairs and over the road and he could soothe the crazy and focus again.

He took off his watch and laid it on the desk next to him. *I don't have to stop drinking forever*, he thought. *Just another ten minutes.*

He opened the file on his computer and focused on what he needed to do. The research team had a lot of objects to sift through for this exhibition, searching for the ones that would be the most effective to convey the desired message. It was about the sexual history of London, a daring subject that skated near some difficult truths about the capital's past. But history didn't have to be portrayed as dry and dusty.

Blake's visions enabled him to see the real people behind the objects, and his job was to help others see them too by putting together insightful curated displays. He loved to bring history to life, giving a glimpse into a past that might inspire others to learn as he had. What better place than the British Museum to do this work? There really was no substitute, so he couldn't lose this job. He just couldn't.

He started typing up his research notes, making suggestions for his specific area. The idea for the exhibition stemmed from the remains of a substantial Roman temple discovered to the south of Southwark Cathedral, with stone foundations and tessellated floors. A jug inscribed with *Londini ad fanus Isidis* – 'In London, at the Temple of Isis' – had been found nearby in 1912, a relic from Roman times.

Southwark back then had been outside the defended area of the Roman city, a no-man's land where any sin could be indulged. There was evidence that Isis, Apollo and Hermes had been celebrated in wild processions culminating in frenzied public orgies on the same land where the cathedral now stood. Every night was Saturday night in Roman Southwark, and alcohol played just as much a part in the lives of the Romans as it did for contemporary Londoners.

Blake forced down his itch for a drink, checking his watch.

Another ten minutes.

He rested gloved hands against a *spintriae*, a Roman brothel token with lists of services for purchase. He wondered what he would see if he tried to read it with bare hands. Would he glimpse the life of the Roman red-light district? Did he want to?

There was a room in the museum that few knew of where he would go to read sometimes. Not read with a book, but with his bare hands, to see into the past of the objects he researched. As much as he considered the visions a curse, he also craved them. Just like the tequila bottle. Was it the lure of the unknown, a break from stifling normality? When he drank, and when he read, Blake didn't know what would happen. Was it about loss of control?

Blake pulled his hand away from the object. He wasn't strong enough to witness what this token might show him this morning. The Romans understood appetite in all its forms: food, sex, violence. All were celebrated to excess in the Roman world. *Perhaps our time is not so different*, Blake thought. *There is such a thin veil of civilization over our animal nature, after all. It takes little to let our teeth show.*

The face of the man upstairs flashed into his mind, and then a memory of the vision in the Nordic forest. The groans of the dying strung up in trees, the grunt of the men who hacked at the corpses, the moon on the dark blood that soaked the earth.

Blake shook his head, banishing the images. He began to search the database for details that would add color to the description of the *spintriae*, attempting to balance the truth with language that would educate but not offend. He tried several different descriptions, chuckling to himself as he wrote, trying for a balance of double-entendre that skirted the edge of acceptability.

As he delved into the archives, he discovered the lists of sexual services were not only displayed on tokens. There were women, known as *bustuariae*, who worked the cemeteries lining the roads out of London. They used gravestones to advertise their services, chalking up their specialty and prices during the day and liaising with clients after sunset. Sex and death were intimately wound together and this could add a new angle to the display.

Blake pulled up the records from the Pompeii exhibition from a few years back, one of the most popular for the museum. The ancient city was the ultimate combination of sex and death, with art depicting satyrs raping animals and gods abusing maidens, where myriad clay penises were dug from the ruins and wall frescoes depicted scenes of orgies. Blake leaned in to type more quickly, the thrill of discovery suppressing his cravings, at least for now.

CHAPTER 5

JAMIE LOOKED MORE CLOSELY at the photograph on the church wall. Magda was clearly a friend of Nick's, their easy camaraderie caught on camera. Jamie knew she should let Missinghall know about the picture, but perhaps this wasn't anything important. After all, both of them worked with people in the community. But maybe it was time to meet Magda Raven officially. Jamie walked back down the nave towards the exit and out into the sun.

Magda wasn't hard to locate. She was a photographer and artist with a studio address listed on her website a block away. Jamie walked down a small alleyway, past the place where the Tabard Inn once stood, where Chaucer's pilgrims had met in the Canterbury Tales. Jamie smiled as she passed the blue plaque marking the spot. It was surrounded by scaffolding from building works in an area that was forever being reincarnated, with layer upon layer of history and life. This was one of the charms of living in London. Every square inch was saturated with history and the echoes of the past could be felt in every footstep.

The building ahead was an old warehouse converted into studio flats. It looked to be mixed industrial and residential, a working artists' haven. The main door had buttons with labelled names and businesses. Jamie rang Magda's bell, and a minute later the intercom crackled.

"Magda's Art. Can I help you?"

"Hi," Jamie said. "I'm new to the community and I was on the walk last night. My name's Jamie Brooke. I wondered if I could talk to you about it."

There was a pause and the sound of a brief muted conversation, before Magda replied.

"Last night was terrible. I don't really know what to say about it, but of course, come in."

The door buzzed and Jamie pushed inside. The corridor was bare, concrete walls presenting a neutral face to the outsider. There were sounds of banging upstairs and the faint tinkle of a piano. A door at the end of the corridor opened to a bright space beyond. Magda Raven stood in the doorway, a tentative smile on her face. She wore a black t-shirt with butterflies all over it and blue jeans over bare feet.

"Come on in," Magda said. "Kettle's on."

The studio was spacious, with a high ceiling supported by metal beams. A row of rectangular windows allowed light to penetrate the space. A stepladder with a wide platform stood underneath one open window, a pair of binoculars and notepad resting on top. There were doors at the other end of the room, one open to give a glimpse of a kitchen. On one side of the studio, white panels separated part of the space, with cameras on tripods and distinctive silver umbrella flash lighting set up. Jamie could see a shadow moving in the space beyond.

"I'm in the middle of an impromptu photo shoot but we're on a tea break right now. Why don't you have a look around?" Magda said. "Would you like tea or coffee?"

"Coffee would be great," Jamie said. "Black, one sugar, please."

Oversize prints covered the studio walls, grouped by theme. Faces of Southwark residents captured in stark black and white, an old woman with wrinkles as deep as scars, a Rastafarian with dreads swinging, smoke wreathed around his head. A young woman leaned against a brick wall, cigarette in her hand, figure-hugging dress revealing slim curves. Her posture invited attention, but her eyes were haunted and cynical.

Birds dominated the next set of prints. Some whirled above the backdrop of the City, silhouetted against the stark outline of the Tower of London. A murmuration of swallows swooped above Stonehenge, a cloud of synchronized beauty in the beginnings of a storm. Then there were close-ups of the ravens Magda had tattooed on her skin, their feathers glossy blue-black, eyes bright. The final panel contained a series of prints in full color, scenes of the Borough streets that brought a smile to Jamie's face with their optimism. Red balloons against the white backdrop of the Globe Theatre. Street performers outside the Tate Modern striking poses for the passing tourists. The silver arc of the Millennium Bridge across the Thames with St Paul's haloed by a sunbeam. The multi-colored ribbons tied to the gates of Cross Bones Graveyard.

There was a corkboard next to the prints, covered in fliers about local events: a masquerade ball, the London Tattoo Convention, and exhibitions coming soon at the British Museum. Jamie's mind flashed to Blake and she wondered what he was working on at the moment.

"See anything you like?" Magda said as she handed Jamie a mug of hot coffee, waving her hand to encompass her prints.

"They're all beautiful." Jamie pointed at the picture of the ribbons. "Cross Bones must mean a lot to you."

"Last night …" Magda shook her head. "Well, I hope that last night wasn't the last memorial there, but the trauma of seeing what we did might mean we have to cancel it for a while." She looked at Jamie more closely. "You're the woman who went to the body."

Jamie nodded. "I used to be a police officer, so I'm used

to crime scenes." Jamie noted that Magda's body stiffened at her words. "But I'm a private investigator these days and I'm not involved in the investigation into the murder. That's with the police now. I recently moved to Southwark, so I'm keen to get to know the community. That's why I came along last night."

"I'm sorry your first experience here was so memorable for all the wrong reasons. But this community is a rainbow of people, which means we have dark as well as light on the spectrum." Magda pointed at the wall of images. "It's not possible to have life without the shadow side."

"Did you know –"

Jamie's question was cut off by a voice from behind the screen.

"Where's my tea, Magda? I'm parched."

O emerged from behind the screen, pulling a sarong around her body to cover her nakedness. Her elfin features were highlighted by dramatic eye makeup, as black as the tattoo under her clothes and emphasized by her ash-blonde cropped hair. Her eyes widened as she caught sight of Jamie.

"I remember you," she said, coming closer. "Last year when Jenna Neville died, you came to the club. What are you doing here?"

Jamie was disarmed by seeing her there. O had broken through her defenses that night at Torture Garden. She had helped with a clue to the case, but also saw through Jamie's professional veneer to the pain beneath.

"I … I've moved here actually. I was there last night. I wanted to see if there was anything I could do."

O came closer, her eyes fixed on Jamie's. "Does death follow you, Jamie Brooke?" O whispered. "Or do you seek it out?"

Jamie couldn't speak. The words were too close to her own thoughts. O broke the moment with a dramatic half turn.

"Why don't you stay while we finish the photo shoot?"

she said. "We're trying to counter the images of death with life. Magda is a fantastic artist."

"Only because you're such a great model to work with," Magda replied with a laugh.

O walked back to the set, unwound her sarong and dropped it to the floor, completely at ease in her naked state. Jamie had seen her tattoo before when O had danced at the Torture Garden nightclub, but in the daylight, it seemed more unusual. Her back was inked with the head of an octopus with tentacles that stretched out to wrap around her slight frame. As she walked in front of the camera, the octopus moved with her, part of her spinal cord.

One tentacle wound up onto her skull, the black visible under short hair, another wrapped around her waist and dipped down between her buttocks. O turned to face the camera and Jamie couldn't help but gaze at how the tentacles of the creature roved across her body. Her breasts were encircled, with one nipple caressed by the creature, while another tentacle wound down between her legs, touching her hairless sex as it penetrated her there. The detail was exquisite and it was incredible to consider the hours of work involved in the entire piece. O was a work of art and her body the canvas. She stamped her originality on the world with her ink, and Jamie wondered if she could ever be as brave herself.

"How do you want me, Magda?" O asked, and there was a trace of flirtation in her voice. Magda walked round in front of the camera and turned O, her fingers lingering on the woman's shoulder, caressing her skin.

"Look up towards the window. We're going for angelic in the next shots."

"A fallen angel, perhaps." O laughed, her cornflower-blue eyes bright. She composed herself and stood as a statue while Magda clicked away.

Every few seconds, O shifted her posture slightly,

changing the angle of her head or her limbs. Her dancing at the Torture Garden had been explicitly erotic, an invitation to sin in a venue that celebrated the physical and the unusual. But here, her body was an embodiment of creation, of human perfection, and the tattoo seemed only to emphasize her vulnerability. Jamie wanted to know why O had chosen this design. Now their paths had crossed again, perhaps she would be able to find out.

Eventually, Magda put the camera down, her face relaxing from the taut posture of the concentrated artist.

"We're done," she said. "There are some great shots in there."

O looked up out of the window, suddenly pointing.

"Look, Magda, the ravens!"

Magda spun quickly and climbed the stepladder up to the high window, gazing out at the birds above, transfixed by their flight. She pushed open the window and began to whistle, soft notes that lilted with a Celtic refrain. It would seem impossible for the tune to be heard above the din of the city and the wind that swept Southwark, but the ravens began to wheel closer.

Magda's song was like a silken cord, drawing the birds to her, and soon there were hundreds of them flying close to the studio windows, their dark eyes fixed on the woman who sang within.

There was a vibration in the air, a heightened sense of connection to the natural world, something Jamie hadn't felt so strongly before in London. It was as if the wild had been brought in here, the rhythms of a far older world reasserting themselves in this cornered civilization. Magda finished her song and threw her arms wide on the final note, the ravens cawing as they winged away and the sky was clear again.

"The ravens are my totem," Magda said, her eyes dark as she descended the ladder. She pulled up her sleeve to reveal the tattoos on her arm in more detail. "They are on me and in me, and they channel my deeper connection to the city."

"I've heard you called an urban shaman," Jamie said. "Is that to do with the ravens?"

Magda smiled. "If I see beyond the skin of the city, then my sight is from the birds. But mainly I live in the world of the practical and human. Like last night."

"Did you know the victim, Nicholas Randolph?" Jamie asked.

"I didn't recognize his body at first. I didn't know it was him ..." Magda sighed. "Nick was a friend and we worked alongside each other. He used to work the streets himself years ago, before finding the church. He was gay and spent a lot of time helping the young male prostitutes. He didn't judge them, but helped them with health issues, education, even with places to stay when they were desperate. He visited them in hospital if they got beaten up. He bought their meds. He was a bloody saint and he didn't deserve to die like that."

"But despite his good works, people judged him as they judge the rest of us," O said. "Especially the Society, those bastards who marched behind us last night." She shook her head. "Suppression of Vice – it's a crazy aim, especially around here. The sex trade has been in this borough since Roman times, through medieval London and up to today. The Society tell themselves that they're trying to save us, but they're really trying to get us to conform."

O pulled on her clothes. Skinny jeans and a man's shirt soon covered her tattoo and she could easily pass for an art student on the street. Then she turned around sharply, her face set in determination.

"Tell her, Magda," she said quietly.

CHAPTER 6

MAGDA SIGHED, HER FACE suddenly looking much older.

"Nick's murder is just the latest in a series of worrying events. There've been a number of people going missing round here recently. Sex workers, illegal immigrants, homeless people. Not exactly the cream of society, but people from our community." Magda paused for a moment to take a sip of her coffee. "Of course these things happen everywhere, but this area is under development and many in power want us gone. Since the Shard was built, prices have shot up and there's a lot of money to be made round here," she said, referring to the 87 story skyscraper in Southwark that opened in 2012 and was still under construction. "If only they can get rid of the deviants, the misfits, those of us who don't fit their idea of the future borough."

"If we're gone," O said, "then they can pretend it's all hipsters and expensive coffee and build luxury flats over the sins of the past."

"What have the police been doing about the disappearances?" Jamie asked.

"We report all of them," Magda said. "But missing persons aren't unusual in these transient lines of work, apparently."

Jamie nodded, understanding the other side. The police

didn't have the resources to tackle every MISPER in London.

Magda looked at her watch. "I've got to head along South Bank for a meeting at the Tate Modern. If you want to walk with me, I'll show you where some of the people disappeared from as we walk."

"I'll come along too," O said. "I'm heading in that direction."

They left the studio and walked back towards Borough Market, turning down Southwark Street and then into Maiden Lane. Neat terraced houses were interspersed with old converted warehouses as they approached the river.

"This was one of the main streets for prostitutes," Magda said, "back when the Globe and the Rose theatres were the center of the red-light district. Bankside was the Elizabethan Soho. If you look at maps of London, you can tell the areas where sex was for sale, although the street names are changed to something more genteel now, of course."

They walked down to the Anchor pub on Bankside, now flanked by a Premier Inn. The budget accommodation seemed appropriate to the history of the area, a place that a modern Chaucer's pilgrims might stay. Magda pointed to a service doorway round the side of the Anchor.

"A friend of ours, Milo, used to sleep rough here," she said. "He disappeared about a month ago. He preferred sleeping out to the hostels where he'd just get bothered." She smiled, her features soft in reminiscence. "He had the face of a fallen Greek god. I've got some photos of him back at the studio."

"He also had a gorgeous back tattoo," O said. "We compared ink one time. He loved dragons and they flew over his skin, scaled in hues of purple and orange flame."

"And you've never heard what happened to him?" Jamie asked.

Magda shook her head. "He's not the only one, and with Nick's murder, I'm worried that Milo may have ended up the same way." She pointed up at the Anchor pub. "The location echoes with Nick's murder, too. The Anchor used to be a brothel and a tavern, a popular place near the bear-baiting pits round the corner in Bear Gardens."

"The Stews," O said. "That's what they called this area. And it's only a block from here to the Palace of Winchester, where the Bishop who licensed the whores sat in luxury. For four hundred years, it was the Bishop's right to exploit the brothels here, and many of London's most attractive architecture is built on the proceeds of the sex trade."

Magda laughed, a hollow sound that reflected the irony of the past. "For all its official line on celibacy and prudery, the church turned a blind eye to prostitution, believing it to be something that would always be part of life. As Saint Augustine said, 'Suppress prostitution and capricious lusts will overthrow society.'"

They walked down a little further to stand on the banks of the Thames. The waters ran swift today, in hues of grey and brown. A working river for trade and commerce, as fast as the city itself, taking goods to the world.

As they continued on, Magda gazed over to the towers and high-rise office blocks on the north bank.

"Look at the City over there. A square mile of conformity, where they slander us by day and then come to play here by night."

She pointed up at a carved stone head with two faces, one pointing east towards the sea and the other west towards the interior of England.

"It's Janus, the god of two faces," Magda said. "A perfect metaphor for London."

Jamie understood the dichotomy. London was both sinner and saint. It was glamorous and gorgeous, a rich and intoxicating pleasure garden. But there was also dirt here and darkness and the stink of rotten dead, the wretched mad and crazy drunks lying in its gutters.

Magda turned to face Jamie, her eyes soft. "This is where the women of the outcast borough have always walked, where men have sinned upon them through sex and lies and judgement. But the earth beneath us and the river that flows through here has nourished us for generations. Someone or some group is trying to move us on, trying to sweep the darkness under the carpet and pretend we don't exist. That's why people are disappearing. But we're not going anywhere."

They continued west along Bankside, the south bank of the river, a popular path with tourists and locals alike. Every time Jamie walked here, her love for the city was renewed. She had been offered a job in the police far away from the city after Polly died. But this was her home now and what was happening in Southwark made her even more sure of her place here. London could rip you up and spit you out and leave you with nothing, but then you wanted more of it. And Jamie craved that edge.

A violinist played in the underpass under Southwark Bridge, the sweet strains of music filling the confined space. O gave a little twirl and put some change in the violin case, blowing the young man a kiss as she did so. There were posters for a masquerade ball pasted along the underpass walls, emblazoned with coquettish eyes peering out from colorful masks.

"You must come to the ball, Jamie," O said. "We're all going and it's going to be such fun. It's a fundraiser for cleaning up Southwark and a number of the Mayoral candidates will be there."

Jamie thought of her nights at tango, a side she had kept away from her professional life in the past. Perhaps it was time that she integrated both into her new life.

"I'll be sure to get a ticket," she said.

They emerged out of the underpass into the sun and walked a little further to the replica of Shakespeare's Globe, a magnet for tourists who snapped pictures against the backdrop of the round, white theatre.

"This was a popular place in medieval times to pick up customers," O said. She flashed a flirtatious smile at a handsome young tourist. "Perhaps it still is ..."

Jamie still wasn't certain what O did. The police side of her was ready to ask, but another part wanted to encourage friendship. In the end, curiosity overcame politeness.

"Do you ..."

Jamie's words trailed off but O picked up the meaning.

"Sell sex?" O said, her eyebrows raised. She appraised Jamie for a moment, as if weighing trust. "Does it matter?"

Jamie shook her head. "No, not at all. I've seen you dance and I would think you'd have people queuing up after that."

Magda grinned. "That she does – but you're picky, aren't you, O?"

They stood for a moment looking out at the Millennium Bridge, a silver parabola that spanned the Thames between the Tate Modern and St Paul's in the City. Tourists walked over it, their footsteps and happy laughter filling the air.

"I used to do a lot more," O said, "but most of my income is from dancing and modeling these days. I still have a few regulars and of course I campaign for better safety. The situation is crazy right now. It's legal to buy or sell sex, but it's illegal for women to join together in a brothel. So we can't practice safely together, we can't get security to protect ourselves from the nut-jobs who inevitably try it on. Sex work is just another kind of work after all, and we should all be safe in our jobs." Her face softened. "Most customers aren't too bad, though."

Magda stretched out her tattooed arm displaying the image of Mary Magdalene kneeling in front of Christ in the garden of Gethsemane. The reformed prostitute as the devoted servant of God.

"Many of my previous clients wanted to cuddle," she said. "To be touched by another person. They were lonely."

"Why did you give it up?" Jamie asked.

"I'm called for other things now," Magda said. "But I know how it feels to be treated the way these women are by a society that can't do without them. It's important for our community to accept the freak and the stranger." She touched the face of Mary on her arm. "The sinners."

"Who is the sinner, anyway?" O said, indicating St Paul's with a nod of her head. "Did you know that the lanes around there are some of the best pickings for the boys?"

O looked at her watch. "Right, I've gotta get to the Kitchen or I'll be late for my shift. When can I see the photos, Magda?"

"I'll have the edits for you tomorrow morning if you want to come over then?"

"Great." O leaned in and kissed Magda on the cheek.

"Can I come to the Kitchen with you?" Jamie asked. "I've heard a bit about it, but I've not been down there yet."

"Sure." O smiled. "We're always in need of a helping hand."

CHAPTER 7

THEY WALKED A COUPLE of blocks into a warren of streets near Mint Street Park, finally reaching a rundown warehouse in a cul-de-sac.

"It's not much, but we try to look after our own round here," O said as she pushed open the back door and stepped into the Kitchen. Jamie followed her inside to find a storage area, shelves stacked high with tinned goods, all labeled and ordered by date. Many were over the sell-by date and O caught Jamie's sideways glance.

"We get a lot of the tins from supermarkets when they go over date," she said. "But there's a period when the stuff inside is still fine. The food bank gives out specific rations, but then we let people take what they want from the over-date bin. Sometimes that makes all the difference." She pointed at a tin of sticky toffee pudding. "I mean, come on, what's not to like about that?"

O laughed, a silvery sound that lifted the dank atmosphere of a place set up to feed the increasing number of poverty-stricken Londoners. She led the way into a commercial kitchen area where several other women had already started work. They called greetings to O as she passed.

"Can you help Meg with chopping vegetables? We've got to get the stew on." O pointed Jamie towards an older black woman with dreadlocks tied back in a blue patterned scarf. She stood by a large sink with a mountain of potatoes in front of her and a box of carrots and other mixed veg next to it.

"Of course." Jamie headed over and introduced herself, grabbed a peeler, and started on peeling the carrots. Although tentative at first, Jamie was soon into a rhythm. There was a meditative state in food preparation, a repetition that left the mind free to wander.

"This stew is for the evening run," Meg said. "It's best to cook it for a long time to soften the offcuts of meat that we get, so we have to start cooking it soon. We get a load of regulars every night and then we take any leftovers out into the parks round here." She smiled and Jamie saw that her teeth were crooked and bent. The wrinkles in her skin were deeper than a woman of her age should have and there were faint scars around her neck. Meg put down her knife and Jamie noticed her hands shaking, perhaps a symptom of long-term alcohol abuse.

"For some who sleep rough, it's their only meal of the day." Meg pointed to a number of round mixing bowls on the side, covered in tea towels. "That's bread, too – we make it ourselves. We have an allotment out east. That green veg is from our garden." There was a quiet pride in Meg's voice and Jamie wondered about her past. Her own tragedy was just one voice in a city of hurt and sometimes it was good to get some perspective, to realize how much others suffered too. Everyone dealt with life in their own way.

O's laugh rippled through the kitchen area and Meg looked up.

"She's magic, that one," she said. "Keeps everyone's spirits up, even when we're overrun. She can bring a smile to the most depressed of our clients, and I've seen her face down a huge man high on meth. She's fearless."

Jamie watched O as she organized the various teams with

a smile and a personal touch that left people beaming. She made them laugh with light remarks, always remembering their names. Jamie thought how different this place was from the police, how isolated she had been there. Her own independence had been partly to blame, but as a woman in a male-dominated environment, she had definitely felt left out. But here she might find a place in a community that really seemed to care for its people.

"Time, everyone," O called out and went to the front door, unlocking it to allow a stream of people into the front area, set up with long tables and benches. They had clearly been queuing outside and they knew the drill. They were quiet as they came in, taking a bowl and lining up for thick porridge liberally doused in white sugar.

One woman with cardboard pieces tied around her body hefted her plastic bags into one corner and stood silently in line.

An old black man shuffled forward with little steps, his gait evidence of Parkinson's, his hands shaking as he reached for a bowl.

A waif of a girl slid through the door, a dirty denim jacket over a short dress, her arms wrapped around herself for warmth. Her eyes were black with kohl and darted around with nervous energy, her movements jerky and jolting.

The smell of unwashed bodies pervaded the cooking area, but no one reacted to it. Jamie supposed it was nothing unusual here. She finished the carrots and began chopping the bunches of green leafy veg. Meg pulled two huge saucepans from a rack and began browning onions and garlic, her shaking diminished as she concentrated on working.

O served strong instant coffee from a big vat, handing it to each person with a smile and a welcome. There was no judgement in her eyes as she looked at them, and Jamie saw that her respect gave the homeless more dignity. They walked to the benches a little straighter in posture, their humanity restored even for a brief moment. Jamie had seen the other side of poverty in the police: the crime and domestic abuse that often resulted from money problems. She had seen these people as criminals, but O and her team saw them as people needing food, warmth and a community.

After everyone had been served, O went around the benches, speaking in low tones to each person. She carried a bunch of leaflets, clearly trying to help with advice as well as food. The waif-like girl kept her head down as O approached, turning her face away. But O sat down next to her, whispering soft words and after a few minutes, the girl reached out a hand and took a leaflet about the sexual health services she could access.

The breakfast service soon finished and as each person left, a young man on the door gave each one a brown bag. He had a blue streak in his blond hair and Jamie recognized him as the guitar player from the Cross Bones memorial. Some people snatched the bag away without thanking him, but others were effusive in their gratitude. One woman had tears in her eyes as she left, clutching the bag close to her chest as she walked out into the day.

"Right, let's get the benches to the side and start weighing out today's rations." O rallied the team as Jamie helped Meg add the meat to the pans and begin to brown them, adding some oregano and other herbs. A delicious smell began to waft through the warehouse, drowning out the unwashed stench that still lingered. The smell of cooking reminded Jamie of the opulence of Borough Market, where food carts overflowed with amazing produce at prices only few could afford. This place was just a few streets away and yet here, they were scraping the barrel to feed the hungry.

"We can't give people anything they want," Meg said, noting Jamie's interest in the rationing preparations. "There are rules for the food bank and we have to weigh out rations for people who come to make sure there's enough for all. We give them three days' emergency food based on the stamps that they bring for themselves and their families." Meg shook her head, a look of despair on her face. "Problem is that some days we don't have enough food here to feed all who come. Makes you wonder, don't it?"

O organized the packing of boxes, some with more perishable food in them than others. Jamie knew that some families didn't even have a way to cook, so there was a balance of tins to whatever fresh food they could get hold of. O made sure to add a couple of apples to each box and Jamie noticed her frown as she surveyed the room, a shadow crossing her beautiful face as she calculated what they had left.

Meg crumbled some stock cubes over the meat, added salt, and poured in a kettle of hot water on top of each pan, then covered them with lids.

"We'll let these simmer for a while now," she said. "I'll get the bread on. Why don't you go help pack boxes? I can manage here."

Jamie walked through the kitchen area and joined in the packing production line, finding a place next to the young man who had been on the door.

"First day?" he asked Jamie, as he added a tin of beans to a box before passing it on to her. Jamie added a packet of macaroni cheese and passed the box to the next woman.

"I guess so," Jamie said, realizing that she would come back here. Looking at the Kitchen made her doubly grateful for what she did have, and she knew that it was only luck and circumstance that put her on this side of the fence.

"We have our ups and downs," the young man said. "Some days we win and we feed everyone. Other days one of our regulars doesn't show up and we hear of suicide or death in the streets. But Southwark is our community and this is our way of caring." He smiled at Jamie. "This place saved me, that's for sure."

O stepped up to the table, a broad grin on her face.

"Ed is one of our regulars. He's a superstar." Ed blushed under O's praise and Jamie saw a glimmer of the unspoiled youth beneath his harder exterior. O brought that out in people. "How are you finding it, Jamie?"

"I'm amazed at everything you do here," Jamie said. "I had no idea, honestly. I'd love to come and help again."

O smiled. "We'd love to have you back." She looked at her watch. "Ten minutes," she called across the room and everyone on the line speeded up their box packing. "Hungry people incoming. Let's feed them all today."

CHAPTER 8

"WE HAVE TO SHUT down that soup kitchen," Mrs Emilia Wynne-Jones said, clutching her designer purse to her chest like a shield as she stood to speak. "It's a danger to the schoolchildren who walk that route every day. And all those homeless beggars …" She shook her head. "One of them might harm a child, because they're probably sex offenders, you know. It's criminal to let them sleep there."

"Not to mention that it's affecting the house prices in the area," one of the older men in the hall said with a grunt, thumping his walking stick on the ground for emphasis.

The church hall echoed with murmurs of assent as the gathered crowd shifted on their seats. The tabled agenda had been finished and now they were onto Any Other Business, which usually consisted of a litany of complaints.

Detective Superintendent Dale Cameron nodded, his face serious as he met the eyes of the complainants. He always enjoyed the meetings of the Society for the Suppression of Vice. They were full of his kind of people, those who were ready to take the hard decisions necessary to make the city great again. After years of focused ambition, his day job was finally taking him into a position of real power.

He looked out at the crowd in front of him – the older stalwarts near the front, middle-aged men and women who voted to get rid of immigrants and return Britain to the white paradise they believed could exist in a multicultural world. Towards the back were a younger group, men with shorn heads and thick-soled boots, hands deep in pockets and wary eyes. They brought physical energy to the old who gathered to complain every week. They were the ones Dale Cameron really aimed to inspire. Men who only looked for a leader to give them permission to act.

Dale nodded at the discussion, his face set with concentration as he listened with one part of his brain even as the other dissected the crowd. He was aware of the impression he made on them. He exuded confidence and control, and years of studying body language had given him an ability to change his behavior to manipulate any situation. With his salt and pepper hair and trim runner's body, he looked more like a corporate CEO than a senior police officer. Not that he expected to be in the police for much longer. He was running for Mayor and fully intended to win.

As the discussion tapered off, he held up his hand for quiet. His authority silenced the room in seconds.

"You all know that I stand for cleaning up the city," Dale said, his voice strong and well measured. "That includes moving the homeless out of the central areas and into communities further away. There's plenty of council housing up north, if we can only get people to accept it."

"Ungrateful little –"

"What are you going to do about the sex workers?"

"When are you going to develop Cross Bones?"

"How will you deal with the drug problems of Southwark?"

Dale held up a hand again, calming the barrage of questions.

"I share the concerns of the Society," he said. "But I can only act with a mandate as Mayor. City Hall is around the corner, so it makes sense that my first acts will be cleaning up my own borough."

"Hear, hear," someone shouted, and Dale smiled out into the crowd. He made eye contact with many of them as applause rang out around the church hall. As they clapped, a ray of sunshine split into myriad colors on the floor, filtered by the brilliant stained glass windows above. Jesus fed the five thousand in one window and healed the blind on another. Dale found himself thinking of Borough Market round the corner. These days, Jesus would probably have to feed the hungry with multigrain spelt bread and wild salmon, that's how entitled they all were.

"You can help drive out the sex workers and the drug addicts," Dale said, and his eyes met those of the hard men at the back. "Report them to the police. Make it difficult for them to work. Make life more unpleasant for them and they will move on – or go back to their own countries."

The applause began again, and then it was time for tea. A queue formed in front of the dais of those who wanted a little one-on-one time with Dale. He would give them all the time they wanted, understanding that every individual connection was one more vote for him in the Mayoral election. His campaign manager was right – it was all about 'high touch.'

As his team organized the line, Dale accepted a china cup of tea from a frail old woman. Her liver-spotted hands shook as she handed it to him. Her eyes were rheumy and her skin sagging around a face that had witnessed the cultural change of the city since the Second World War.

"It's good that you're here, love," she said. "None of those other politicians understand that we have to reclaim what belongs to us before it's too late. It's time to stamp out the cockroaches and you're the man to do it." She patted Dale's shoulder and shuffled away, leaving him to ruminate on the surprising nature of some of the members.

The Society for the Suppression of Vice had been started in the nineteenth century to promote public morality, a successor to the Society for the Reformation of Manners. Dale liked the overtones of the word reformation, but manners were something few cared about and didn't quite have the dramatic ring to it. But who could object to the suppression of vice, a word that conjured all the nasty, dirty things that went on under cover of darkness. Surely no one could openly support those making money from vice – the prostitutes, the drug pushers, the criminals. Who would stand for them? Of course, Dale thought, as he took another sip of his tea, such obvious vice was merely the thin end of the wedge. He wouldn't rest until the city was clean in all senses of the word.

His idea of a future London centered around the temple of Salt Lake City, a beacon of shining white against a backdrop of blue. Not because of faith, but because of those who looked to it as the pinnacle of good behavior and of perfect obedience.

Whereas London ... Dale shook his head as he stirred his tea. Well, London had been a melting pot of multiculturalism, artistic expression and personal freedom for far too long. The Society sought to redress the balance and take back the city for morality – pushing a right-wing agenda that would move the poor on benefits out of the city, clean up the streets of hookers and drug pushers, scrub the stain of graffiti from the walls of Shoreditch and Hoxton and renew a sense of pride in the city.

One of the younger men from the back approached and Dale waved him forward. The man sat opposite him and leaned closer. His jaw was much larger on the left than on the right, an asymmetry that Dale tried not to stare at. The man smelled of tobacco smoke and fried bacon. The thought of a breakfast fry-up made Dale's stomach rumble.

"There's some of us that want to help with your campaign," the man said. "We work out at the boxing gyms in South London and there's a lot of support for what you want to do. If you need us, give me a call. Here's my card."

The man handed over a business card with frayed edges and a blue boxing glove in the middle. Dale took it, noting the scars on the man's knuckles.

"Thank you, I appreciate the offer. There will definitely be leafleting to be done over the coming weeks." Dale met the man's steel gaze and saw that they understood each other. "I'll have my office call you."

They shook hands and the man walked off without looking back.

A well-preserved middle-aged woman sat down next, her designer outfit coordinated in shades of camel and ivory. She placed her knees together, her slim legs and high-heeled shoes tucked under the chair. She placed her hands in her lap, manicured nails with a hint of natural color. A large diamond sparkled on her left hand alongside a gold wedding band. Dale noticed how soft her hands looked and he wondered briefly how they would feel on his skin.

"Detective Superintendent –" she began, her eyes darting to his.

"Dale, please," he said, putting a hand briefly on her knee. She colored a little and raised a hand to her neck, touching the pulse point there.

"Oh. Dale, then." She smiled and he saw opportunity in her gaze. Flirting was always a good way to get another vote.

"I'm part of a group within the church," she said. "We're trying to encourage the sex workers into an abstinence program. We've had some success, but we'd like to get official backing from the Mayor's office. Perhaps even some funding?"

Dale smiled, pouring sincerity into his gaze.

"Of course, that's the kind of program I'd like to encourage. Once I'm elected, I'd appreciate it if you could submit your proposal to my office. I will personally make sure it gets the proper attention."

"Thank you," the woman said, her smile wider now. "Our

aim is to honor what the original Society intended."

Dale knew that the Society had been formed by William Wilberforce in order to stem the immorality so rife in the Georgian period, when prostitution added almost as much to the economy as the thriving London Docks. It aimed to ban public drinking, swearing, lewdness and other immoral and dissolute practices, as well as ending the obscenity of pornography and disorderly pubs and brothels. It was a good model for the modern Society. But in Dale's opinion, they had made one mistake that still rippled through the strata of Britain. By banning what they called 'obscene publications,' they had also stopped the distribution of contraceptive advice to the working classes, giving rise to more births amongst the poor.

One of Dale's intentions was to introduce a substantial one-off payment to any woman who underwent sterilization, which would encourage those worse off in society to stop breeding. *About bloody time the class balance was redressed*, he thought. Once the dregs of society were dealt with, then he would start trying to get the right sort of people to have more babies. They would need a working group on how to influence more intelligent women to stop pursuing aggressive careers. It was an unfortunate correlation that the more educated a woman was, the fewer children she had.

"May I have your autograph?" the woman asked, pulling a pad from her handbag. "Once you're Mayor, you'll be far too busy."

She bent forward and Dale caught a trail of her scent in the air. Ponds Cold Cream. His breath caught in his chest and he was back in that room with his mother. As she stroked the cream into his skin, the door had slammed open. His father stood in the doorway, still wearing his police uniform, his face red from drinking after his shift. *You little faggot.* His father's voice had been a growl, an animal sound as he stepped towards them with fists clenched.

He always rolled up his sleeves before he began, revealing the tattoos on his forearms. One arm displayed Justice as a beautiful woman holding a sword in one hand, her weighing scales in the other, blood dripping beneath from her blindfold. The other arm was inked with the words his father lived by: *When justice is done, it brings joy to the righteous but terror to evildoers. Psalm 21:15*. Dale understood his father's right to discipline his family – it was how he felt about London now. After all, spare the rod, spoil the child.

"Are you OK?" the woman asked, her eyes concerned.

"Of course." Dale smiled and refocused on her. "Sorry, it's been a long day already." He pulled a fountain pen with a silver fox-head cap from his inside top pocket. He signed his name with a flourish, realizing that this was likely just the start of such events. Perhaps he would even take a book deal once he was Mayor.

The woman walked off the stage, her hips swaying a little more than was necessary. Dale felt a familiar stirring. He took another sip of his tea and waved for the next person to come forward. He would stay here until he had given them all a moment of his time, but later tonight he would indulge his own particular brand of release.

CHAPTER 9

JAMIE SAT AT HER tiny desk, scanning through the financial records of a husband whose disgruntled wife was sure he was having an affair. Her new office was the size of a large cupboard, rented in a shared office space on the edge of Southwark. She had tried working in her new flat, but surprisingly, she missed having colleagues around. She had never been the chatty type, preferring to keep quiet and rarely drinking with the other police, but there was an energy in having other people around.

The shared office space was a way to get some normality back into her life, the routine of getting out of the flat, looking presentable enough for others not to notice her. The office space was generally quiet, with the tapping of keyboards and low voices making phone calls. She nodded to the other people she saw in the lobby and little kitchen, but she could see reservation in their eyes. She wondered how fast the turnover was round here. Perhaps when she had been here for a while, they would accept her as part of the community – and she did intend to be here a while.

Jamie returned her attention to the records in front of her. From what she could see, the man was having much more than an affair. She'd tracked him to another house and it looked like he had another family altogether. Jamie shook her head. She had barely managed a relationship with one person. Two marriages would be a hell of a lot of work.

She added the last pieces of information to the file, attaching photos of the man's second family. The woman had essentially paid to destroy her marriage, to break apart the status quo. Part of Jamie didn't want to send the information to her client, but perhaps the woman knew already and could use this to move on. Or perhaps she would find strength in her children. A sudden rush of loneliness took Jamie by surprise. She missed Polly every day, but the grief had subsided to a dull ache most days. It was a back note to her life, but this spike was something new. She completed the file, resolving to avoid marital cases if she could. She preferred missing persons – at least they had some chance of a happy ending.

Her mobile phone buzzed and she saw Magda's name on the screen. She picked it up.

"Hi, Magda."

"Jamie." Her voice was broken with concern. "You have to help. You need to come quickly."

"Of course. What's wrong?"

"O's missing. I went over to her flat to show her the photos from yesterday. She didn't answer the door or her phone, so I let myself in with the spare key. Her bed hadn't been slept in. I don't think she's been back here since we were with her yesterday."

Jamie thought of O's dancing at Torture Garden, and her admission of occasional sex work. O was a beautiful woman and there were plenty of possibilities for where she could be.

"Perhaps she was working?" Jamie said.

"No." Magda was emphatic. "We have a check-in system for when she works. If it's sex work or dancing or anything potentially risky, she texts me. Even when it's something fun and casual, she always lets me know. She wouldn't miss that, Jamie. She knows the lifestyle risks and that's how we manage it." Magda's voice was high-pitched with desperation. "She's been taken, I know it."

"Did you report it to the police?" Jamie asked.

"Yes," Magda said, "but I know they're not taking it seriously."

"It's not really been long enough yet for them to consider it a missing person, but I know some people," Jamie said. "What's the address? I'll be there as fast as possible."

After getting the information, Jamie jumped on her motorbike, weaving through the streets until she reached a Victorian terrace behind a park. Magda stood outside smoking, her fingers shaking as she sucked on the cigarette. Her face was pinched with worry. Bare of makeup, she looked much older.

As Jamie put her helmet in the pannier, Magda wiped a tear from her cheek.

"I keep thinking of Nick's body," she said. "Whoever it was cut his tattoos off. Maybe Milo too. What if they have O?"

Jamie thought of how much of O's perfect body was inked, trying not to imagine her skin covered in blood.

"We'll find her," Jamie said. "Show me the flat and then I can call someone. I still have friends in the police."

Jamie followed Magda up the stairs of the terrace into a second-floor flat. The door opened into a large living and dining space, with one side separated into a tiny kitchen. There was a separate small bedroom and postage-stamp-size bathroom. Framed prints decorated the cream walls, all of sea creatures and dominated by octopi. There were several erotic Japanese prints, clear evidence of the inspiration for the intimacy of her tattoo.

The flat was minimalist, in keeping with O's Japanese interest. A futon with white linen and a red pillow dominated the bedroom. It felt empty, and Jamie was sure that Magda was right. O had not slept here last night.

"Do you know where she was going after her shift at the Kitchen?" Jamie asked. "When I left, she was still there."

Magda shook her head. "She mentioned meeting someone to discuss a potential modeling contract, but it was in a coffee shop somewhere, nothing seedy. Her ink sets her apart and she has photographers flocking to take her picture these days."

Jamie went to the window, looking out at the back of other houses in the area. She called Missinghall.

"Al, it's Jamie. Have you got a minute?"

"This murder case is crazy but of course, I'll help if I can."

"It's about a MISPER, a friend of mine. Olivia Ivorson."

There were sounds of typing as Missinghall searched for any notifications.

"Another one in Southwark." His voice was grim. "It's not a great place to be at the moment, Jamie. When did she go missing?"

"Sometime last night. After ten p.m."

More sounds of typing.

"She's a sex worker by the look of it. She's been cautioned before. Maybe she's out working?"

"I know she isn't, Al. And I'm concerned because she's heavily tattooed."

"It's not unusual these days, Jamie. You know that. Most of bloody London has ink now."

Jamie saw O's perfect body in her mind, the alabaster skin claimed by the octopus that encircled her. Jamie shuddered at the thought of a blade drawn over that flesh.

"You said yourself that Southwark isn't a great place to be right now."

Missinghall sighed. "Look, everyone is focused on the Winchester Palace murder right now, but I'll see what I can do."

"OK, thanks, Al. I'll keep looking this end and I'll text you with any updates."

Jamie ended the call and turned to Magda. "I don't think we're going to get any help from the police at the moment. She's got form."

Magda put her head in her hands, her shoulders slumped in defeat.

"There might be another way," Jamie said. "I have a friend who might be able to help. Do you mind if I call him?"

Magda looked up, a glimmer of hope in her eyes. "Please, anything you think. Maybe he can come over?"

Jamie scrolled through her contacts for Blake's number. Her heart raced a little at the thought of his voice and of seeing him again. They had both been through a lot since the events surrounding the murder of psychiatrist Dr Christian Monro. Jamie had seen Blake at his weakest then, and she knew he still struggled to put the mental torture of what he had seen during that case behind him.

Her own decision to leave the police and start a new life meant she had been busy, and they had both kept away from each other. But Jamie knew it was more to do with an instinctive desire not to be hurt. They were both vulnerable, and there was a spark between them that could devastate them both if they gave into it. She remembered the night she had gone to Blake's flat – the night Polly's body had disappeared. He had been high on tequila and she had wanted to lie down next to him, let him sink into her. But he was dangerous. His gift both frightened and intrigued her, but perhaps now it could help her new friends.

She dialed his number.

"Jamie?"

Blake's voice was smooth, and Jamie couldn't help but smile. She had missed him and from his tone, he was pleased to hear from her.

"Hi, Blake, how are you?"

"Busy prepping for a new exhibition," he said, a smile in his voice. "You know the world of academia never stops its frenetic pace. How's your new business?"

"Actually, that's why I'm calling. There's been a disappearance and I could use some help. Any chance you could come have a look?"

There was a moment of silence, and Jamie could picture Blake's handsome face as he wrestled with the decision. The last time she had asked for his help, Blake had ended up drugged and tortured for his gift by men who intended to break his mind and send him into oblivion. She understood his hesitation.

"Is it a murder?" Blake asked, and Jamie heard a note of trepidation in his voice. She turned away, hoping Magda hadn't heard the words.

"I hope not," she said. "A friend has disappeared and the police investigation will be too slow for my liking. But I'm really worried. There have been other disappearances that haven't ended well round here lately. I could really use your help, Blake."

"Where are you?" he asked.

"Southwark," Jamie said, giving him the address.

"I'll come over in the next hour," Blake said. "Extended lunch break."

***

Blake arrived as Jamie made Magda a fourth cup of tea. O's flat had nothing stronger and Magda didn't even drink anymore. Reformed in so many senses of the word, Magda's strength had seemed boundless, but it was clear from her hunched shoulders and staring eyes how much O meant to her.

The doorbell rang and Jamie went down to open it. Blake stood in the doorway, two coffees in his gloved hands, his blue eyes bright.

"I figured you could use some," he said. Jamie stretched up to kiss his cheek, her lips brushing his stubble. He smelled of sandalwood soap and she wanted to lean in to him, feel his arms around her.

"It's good to see you," she said, stepping away.

"You too," Blake replied, and his eyes said all she needed to know.

She took one of the coffees.

"Come on up."

They entered the flat and Magda got up to greet Blake. He indicated the coffee.

"Sorry, I didn't know there was someone else here. Would you like my coffee?"

Magda smiled weakly, worry breaking through her resolve. "If you can help with this," she said, shaking her head. "I'll get you all the coffee you need. What can I do to help?"

Jamie knew Blake would be reluctant to talk about his unusual gift with someone he didn't really know.

"To be honest, Magda," she said. "I think maybe you should go and have a rest. O might even show up at your studio for those photos. We'll be here a while."

Magda nodded. "You're right. I should go." She handed over the keys. "Let me know if you find anything, or if you have any questions." She left the flat, her footsteps heavy on the stair, leaving Jamie and Blake alone.

For a moment, the silence lay between them. There was so much to say and yet, none of it really mattered. Jamie knew the attraction between her and Blake was dangerous, and she needed his friendship more than anything. The balance was difficult to manage, but perhaps this time they could walk the tightrope.

"So, what happened?" Blake asked.

Jamie told him about O and the other disappearances in the area, as well as the murder from the night before.

"We're worried about her," Jamie said. "Her tattoo makes her fit the profile of the other victims."

Blake looked around the flat.

"So you want to know where she might be?"

"Anything you can help with really. Perhaps there's something in here that might give us some clues as to where she is."

CHAPTER 10

BLAKE LOOKED AROUND THE small flat, traces of a woman he didn't know yet in the furnishings and pictures on the walls. He usually read objects where the memories of those entwined with them were dead and gone, the civilizations they came from crumbled and fallen. But this woman, Olivia, might come home any minute and it made him anxious.

The last time he had read a living person, it was the day of his father's death. He had seen demons consume the frail body and that had sent him over the edge into his own madness. But that's why he was here. He still owed Jamie for rescuing him from the delirium of the RAIN experiments. If she needed to know what was going on, then he had to help, even if it put his job in jeopardy.

He looked at his watch. He could still get back within the hour if they were quick.

While Jamie began to search the living room area, Blake walked through into O's bedroom and sat down on the futon, looking around the small bedroom for a sense of what O valued most, for what might give him insight into her life.

He looked down to the side of the bed at a low table with a lamp on it. There was a jade greenstone pendant lying there, shaped in a Maori *manaia* design. With the head of a bird, a human body and the tail of a fish, the *manaia* was the messenger of the gods, representing spiritual power and a guide beyond the physical realm. The frayed leather cord tied around the neck of the bird indicated that O wore this often. Something about it called to Blake and he could almost feel the smooth stone in his palm.

He took off his gloves and picked up the pendant with bare hands. The crisscross network of scars didn't prevent him from feeling the coolness of the jade and the contours fitted into his hand perfectly. His heart raced a little in a combination of fear at what might come but also exhilaration at glimpsing into another's world. He closed his eyes and let the visions come.

The mists of memory swirled about him and Blake sensed many emotional threads tied around this one pendant, but there was one that was particularly strong. He let himself sink into that layer of consciousness and opened himself up to the sensation.

He was weightless, floating in a blue-green ocean, experiencing a scuba dive as O had done one day when she had worn the pendant. Blake heard the rhythmic sound of her deep breathing through the regulator, watched the bubbles float away and, for a moment, he understood why people craved time underwater.

He could feel O's calm, her almost meditative state as she finned above a rocky bottom. It was cool and he could feel the thickness of the wetsuit she wore. These were temperate waters, not a warm coral paradise. Mats of thick kelp covered the walls and rocks around, swaying in the surge. Wrasse in shades of purple and green darted in and away, curious of the diver, while blue two-spot demoiselles clustered in the shelter of the kelp.

O leaned forward, tipping over to descend, exhaling to empty her lungs. Her buoyancy control was natural and her body relaxed, as if she were part of this aquatic realm, unhindered by the heaviness of the gear she wore. A hole in the rocks appeared as she descended and she finned towards it, heading into a sea cave.

It was dark inside but Blake sensed no fear in her. She added a little air and then floated, neutrally buoyant.

Blake felt another presence, something substantial, something powerful. His eyes adjusted to the dark and shapes appeared in the cave. There were boulders on the bottom, lumps of grey stone covered in soft coral, big-eye fish clustering at the edges of view. Something stirred in the shadows and then moved towards them in the water. O's excitement was palpable but she stayed motionless, waiting for it to come closer.

The octopus ascended, its tentacles hanging below, curling slowly in the water. It was large and covered in nodules, its bulbous head as big as a watermelon. Its eyes were pools of black in the semi-darkness but Blake sensed an intelligence and a curiosity for the creature who entered its territory. It glided past towards the cave entrance and O turned to watch it silhouetted against the light, following slowly after. Its movement was mesmerizing, each tentacle a separate dexterous limb twisting in the blue.

It swam out of the cave and O emerged after it, eyes fixed on its strange beauty. It was inescapably alien, a body with no backbone that could squeeze into the tiniest hole and yet, out here, it was glorious. Blake tried to fix the moment in his mind, the sun shining down through the water patterning on the octopus' skin as it turned in the water to examine the diver in the light. The second stretched on and Blake felt the connection, understood why O was so fascinated with the creature. It was wild and free in this wide ocean, something a human could never be.

The sound of a boat engine rumbled through the water and the octopus shot away incredibly fast, all eight tentacles thrusting, turning its body into a torpedo that sped out of sight. Blake felt O's loss at its disappearance, the moment broken, perhaps never to be repeated. As the intensity of the experience dropped away, the mists of memory began to swirl about him and he reached for tendrils of pain associated with the pendant that were bound to another time and place.

As he fixed on the new vision, it crystallized into a tattoo studio. O lay on her back, the pain intense as the tattoo artist inked a tentacle on the skin under her exposed breast. The man looked up, his brown skin marked with a full facial Maori moko.

"Just say the word, O, and we can take a break."

"I can do another ten minutes," she said, clenching her fists. "We've got to finish it. I'm moving to Europe as soon as we're done."

"I'm going to miss my finest work," the man said, bending his head again. "But maybe I'll see you at the tattoo convention sometime. I've heard they have a good one in London."

The buzz of the tattoo machine started again and Blake could feel the nuances of pain as it inked O's skin. There was a sense of being fully present in her body, a crossing over into a place where thought was secondary to physical sensation. It was an initiation of sorts, where pain represented the crossing of a threshold into a new world. Once crossed, there was no way to remove the mark.

Blake understood now why O wanted to have the octopus on her skin. It represented camouflage and the ability to transform its body in movement. It was grace and intelligence and, ultimately, escape. It had marked her that day in the sea cave and now it would mark her skin until death parted them.

That thought ripped Blake from the vision, for he felt no sense of O's end in the strings of memory. He didn't really understand what the visions meant or how they worked, but he had learned to trust his instinct. O was alive – at least for now.

***

Blake pulled his hand from the pendant and sat for a moment, breathing deeply as he reoriented himself to the surroundings. He looked up at the Japanese octopus print on the wall and smiled. The vision he had seen was a privilege, a glimpse into a world he might never see with his own eyes. Sometimes his psychic ability was a curse, to be drowned in tequila until he could no longer feel. But this was a glimpse into something wonderful, and now he felt such a connection with O that he was determined to help Jamie find her.

He stood up and went back into the living area. Jamie flicked through a pile of papers on a bookshelf and looked up as he came in.

"Find anything?" she asked, then frowned. "Are you OK? You look pale."

Blake held up the pendant. "I read this and at least now I understand her obsession with octopi. I had a brief tattoo experience, as well."

Jamie raised her eyebrows. Blake knew she had been skeptical at first, doubting the veracity of his visions. But after the last two cases they had been involved in, she accepted what he discovered without need for further explanation.

"Did you see anything that could help us find her?"

Blake shook his head. "Nothing concrete, but I think it would make sense to connect with the tattoo community in London. Her ink had deep meaning for her and might bring us closer to finding out where she was last night. Her tattoo artist was Maori and I think I'd recognize him if I saw him again."

Jamie shuffled through the papers on the desk. She held up a printed flier for the London Tattoo Convention and smiled.

"This is a multi-day event and it went on late into last night. Maybe O was there? We could head over now and see what we can find out. Can you spare the time?"

Blake thought of the caution that lay on his desk back at the British Museum, of Margaret's stern expression. He should get back and spend the rest of the day in research. But when he was with Jamie, his craving for alcohol lessened and surely the focus on finding O, a living woman, was more important that investigating those dead and gone.

"I'll file the time under research," he said, with a smile.

**

The Tobacco Dock was an early nineteenth-century warehouse of sturdy brick and ironwork that had once housed imported tobacco. It was in that part of East London described as 'up and coming,' still underdeveloped and affordable but on the edge of turning fashionable. It wouldn't be long before the artists had to move even further out of the city.

"I've thought about getting a tattoo, you know," Jamie said as she and Blake entered the gates into the venue. "I can't decide what I'd want to have done though." She thought of Polly and how her daughter would have liked to help choose the design. There were so many possibilities. But in the end, Jamie knew that her own body carried the memory of her child, her own flesh and blood now turned to dust.

"I'm considering it too," Blake said, pulling Jamie from her thoughts. "When I read O's pendant, I had a glimpse of what ink meant to her and why the octopus is her totem. I'm convinced there will be people here we can ask about her."

The venue separated into several spaces around open courtyards overlooked by a second tier of rooms. There were booths hung with flash, tattoo art displaying the style of the artist from traditional naval styles to curly feminine floral motifs, Chinese dragons and darker tribal marks. A rock band played to a lively crowd, overlaying the sound of buzzing from the tattoo machines. There was sizzling from the barbeques and the smell of roasting meat, hot chips and coffee hung in the air.

A generation ago, there would have been stereotype attendees to these type of events – fat and balding Hell's Angel types, gang members, sailors and prostitutes. A freak show of outcasts, considered deviant by decent people. But now the crowd was mixed, beautiful young women wandering amongst middle-aged rebels sipping Pinot Grigio, and, of course, a healthy dose of leather-clad men, from male model to grandfather. Some art was discreet, a single image on a patch of skin. But others had gone all in, art personified, their bodies a canvas of meaning.

A man walked past wearing plain black jeans and boots, the simplicity setting off his bare torso. There was no patch of skin unmarked by dense tattoos, the images ranging from the head of the Devil at his navel, to a huge dragon around his ribs that wrapped into steampunk wings on his back. His head was shaven and his skull and face were tattooed in strong black geometric shapes.

"With so many inked bodies and tattoo artists, how are we going to find those connected to O?" Blake wondered aloud.

They continued walking through the maze of booths. The buzz of tattoo machines was a soothing backdrop, like bees on a summer's day. Many of the clients lay relaxed under the skilled hands of the artists, trusting their skin to strangers.

"Why do you think tattoos have become so popular these days?" Jamie asked, as they stopped to watch one artist ink script into a man's shaven skull.

"Marking skin is nothing new," Blake said. "The oldest human bodies found in glaciers have tattoos, showing allegiance to a tribe or gang, or to God. Perhaps that's the point. We've lost that sense of meaning in our secular society so we go through ritual behavior in the ultimate pursuit of individualization. Tattoos are only the start – I've read that there's also a rise in piercings, scarification, branding and implants."

Jamie thought of Rowan Day-Conti's extreme body modification from the Jenna Neville case, and his obsession with how the body could be used in life as well as in death. He had been her first connection to O.

The rock music finished and the roar of the crowd subsided. In the brief lull, Jamie heard music that reminded her of the night at the Torture Garden when she had seen O dance.

"This way," she said, heading off in the direction of the music, through the crowds of people as Blake tried to keep up.

CHAPTER 11

THEY EMERGED ON THE second floor overlooking a stage area with a raised dais and a pole that stretched up to the ceiling. A mixed-race woman in a leather bikini hung upside down and as she spun around, Jamie saw her back was a tattooed garden of exotic flowers that curled and bloomed across her skin. It was beautiful, complementing her curves and, judging by the flash of cameras in the audience, much appreciated.

Blake's eyes were fixed on the dancer as she slid around the pole in an acrobatic and sensual display of strength and flexibility. Jamie understood his fascination, because the woman was stunning. She knew that her own release came in tango. She wondered if Blake would look at her like that if she danced for him. But that was a side of her life that she kept private – for now at least.

The music finished and the dancer stepped off the dais to be mobbed by fans asking her to sign photos. Jamie found it interesting that most of these fans were women, many in plain clothes. Perhaps they wanted to find the courage to expose themselves as she did, to ink their skin and be proud of their bodies.

They finally made it to the front of the queue and Jamie introduced herself and Blake.

"We're looking for a friend of ours who has gone missing," she said. "You might know her as O. She has a –"

"Octopus tattoo," the woman said, cutting off Jamie's words. "I know her. She was meant to be here today, part of our performance team, but she didn't show up. There are plenty of girls ready to take her place but she was missed by the fans. She has quite the following from Torture Garden."

"Do you know if her tattooist is here?" Blake asked. He smiled and Jamie watched as the woman melted in the face of his charm. She had to admit that a tiny part of her was jealous, but if they could use his good looks to find O, it was worth it.

The woman leaned closer.

"He is here, actually. All the way from New Zealand. I'm on my break now, so I could take you to him and maybe show you around a bit." She brushed her hair back from her face and touched Blake's arm, looking up into his eyes. "I'm Minx, by the way."

Of course you are, Jamie thought, managing to keep quiet as Blake accepted her offer of help.

Minx led them through a central area reserved for artists engaged in more traditional tattoo methods. A Polynesian man used a small hammer to drive a stick into a man's shoulder. Each stroke was deliberate and the man underneath looked as if he was barely coping with the pain. Yet he remained unmoving, determined to go through this initiation as generations before him had done.

"The word tattoo comes from *tatau* in the Polynesian language," Minx said. "It means to strike and mimics the sound of the hammer hitting the stick. Modern tattooing uses machines, of course. They can do far more pricks per minute than tattooing by hand, but it's all so clinical these days."

Winding through the halls, Minx stopped at a booth dedicated to implants. The walls were covered with objects that could be put under the skin. The man running the booth had a row of beads in his skull, raised bumps like a dinosaur spine. A raised cross implant with bulbous ends sat in the middle of his bare chest, skull tattoos erupting with flame on his pectoral muscles.

"Hey Zee, d'you know where Tem Makaore's stall is?"

Zee turned and his eyes were kind, soft brown like a puppy and Jamie instinctively warmed to him, despite his unusual looks. He bent to kiss Minx's cheek and smiled at Jamie and Blake.

"He's down the back of the vaults 'cos he booked late."

Jamie leaned closer to examine some of the items on show. There were different sizes of horn from little bumps to several inches, as well as thin batons and rings. Zee noticed her interest.

"Skin is remarkable," he said. "You can stretch it over things and it will accommodate. So you can embed a small object at first, a round marble, for example, and the skin will stretch around it. Over time, you replace the small object with a larger one. Or you can have silicone injected to stretch it slowly into shape."

Blake pointed at a row of long metal spikes for skull implants.

"How can you possibly sleep with those in?" he asked.

Zee smiled at the question, keen to talk about his art. "The implants in the skull are actually metallic studs so the spikes can be attached by day and removed at night."

"That's pretty cool," Blake said. "Not sure how well it would go down at the office though."

"People are trying all kinds of things these days," Zee said. "Braille implants for example, to enable blind people to enjoy body modification. There's also a rise in magnetic finger implants which act like another sense. The wearer can feel magnetic fields, from portable electronics to invisible magnetic fields. Split tongues are requested more in these days as dragons have seen a resurgence in interest.

"Ultimately, I'm a skin artist, and the bodies I work with are temples to my god. I create the implants that result in a changed shape. I carve away excess flesh to leave an artwork behind. I restructure to create." He pointed at a photo of an ear reshaped into that of a cat. "Individuation is the point. To be set apart from mundanity. I mean, look at our developed world. How many people are trapped in lives of quiet desperation? I help people escape that through embracing their power. I match the outer body to the inner vision of self."

"It's fascinating," Jamie said. "I hope we have time to come back later."

They walked away from the stall, heading down the stairs towards the vaults.

"Zee's lover died a few years back," Minx said as they descended. "He had the ashes put into that hollow cross and implanted them over his heart."

Her tone was respectful, both of his choice to implant and his method of remembrance. Jamie understood that need to have the dead so close they could not be forgotten, even for an instant. Ashes could be made into glass and diamonds now, turned into tribute jewelry. She had also heard that they could be mixed with ink and used in a tattoo. That thought actually appealed to Jamie. Polly had understood the attraction of the macabre and would have laughed about it.

The vaults level had an eclectic range of stalls ranging from tattoo inks and equipment to a cabinet-of-curiosities shop, selling animal skulls, taxidermy, and art made from human teeth. The buzzing of her cellphone caught Minx's attention and as she answered, she pointed Jamie and Blake towards the back of the vaults, waving them away.

"Maybe you can say goodbye after her next show," Jamie said with a smile as they walked down the corridor.

"I don't think I could keep up with her," Blake grinned. "This place is amazing, though. I keep wondering how much of this will end up in the British Museum eventually, part of British civilization in the twenty-first century. Future academics will be musing over the tribal markings and obscure implants from this age, as they do over ancient peoples."

Several booths hung with Maori and Polynesian designs sat in the corner of the vaults, the distinctive use of white space highlighted in bold black to create *koru* spirals and geometric shapes. It was quieter down here, the sound of the bands muted by thick walls and flooring.

Three men stood near one of the booths, drinking bottles of beer. They turned as Jamie and Blake approached, their faces marked by tribal tattoos, their body language aggressive. Jamie took a deep breath.

CHAPTER 12

"WE'RE LOOKING FOR TEM Makaore," Jamie said, although Blake was clearly looking at one of the men more intently. He had distinctive facial moko, the blue-black ink curving around his chin and jawline, bisecting his nose with geometric shapes, sweeping up from his eyes like the wings of the dawn. His lips were fully tattooed and the fierce markings made him look like a warrior from another time, incongruous against his black t-shirt and jeans. Jamie had a fleeting desire to see if the ink continued on the rest of his tightly muscled body.

"I'm Tem," the man said, his face breaking into a smile. The warrior persona dropped away. "Kia ora. What can I do for you?"

"A friend of ours, O, is missing. We wondered if you'd seen her?"

Tem frowned.

"Of course, I know O. I'm super proud of her ink and I don't get to do such extensive work too often. We met for a drink last night about eight and she was meant to come by today, but I haven't seen her since then."

"We're worried about her," Jamie said. "Did she tell you anything about where she was going after you met?"

"No, but I wouldn't expect her to. But she wanted to talk

DEVIANCE

about new ink, which means something has happened in her life. Something has changed. You see, the soul can't speak in words." Tem smiled, his eyes wistful, and Jamie wondered at the bond between tattoo artist and the skin he worked on. "The soul can only speak in symbols and patterns and every person will choose something different. Or, if they choose the same symbol, the meaning will be different."

"What did she want done?" Jamie asked.

Tem gestured for them to come closer and see some of the designs on the wall of the booth.

"She only had vague ideas and it's bad etiquette to ask the meaning of someone's tattoo," he said. "It's possible that the person themselves won't know what it really means." He pointed to his facial moko. "To try and put these markings into words will lessen their power. But you have to understand that to tattoo or modify your body is to embrace the shadow side of yourself. That's why many can't do it.

"Most people cannot bear to look into that darker side, preferring to keep the mask of normality. But to repress the shadow for too long will mean it eventually has to escape in other ways. Into compulsions, into chaos." Tem looked at Jamie, his dark brown eyes as tangled as an ancient wood. She saw secret things hidden in those depths, a glimpse of an older world. "I think O's octopus has been dominant for too long and to change, she has to ink something new. But I can't tell you what. She wanted to know how long I was in town as we'd need several sessions. But she was ready to walk through the fire again."

Jamie tilted her head to one side, his words puzzling her. "What do you mean by that?"

Tem pointed at the tattooing instrument on the bench. "That is for pain but also for change. After all, nothing worth doing is entirely painless. Friendships fade, marriages break apart, families splinter, but your body is yours until the end. What you do to it will be with you every day until you breathe your last. So you mark your skin to mark the path through the fire of life, and after the change is complete, the wound is bandaged and you can heal."

A picture on the wall drew Jamie's eye. A woman stood side on, her arm lifted to reveal a tattoo that opened up the inside of her body as if she were clockwork. Behind broken ribs, cogs and wheels turned, pistons pumped and over them lay a network of bones and skin. It was a macabre optical illusion of a steampunk hybrid. Next to her was a woman with blonde hair, her dark eyes staring into the camera from a face of blue and purple swirls, her whole body encased in ink.

"She was born with a skin condition," Tem said, noticing Jamie's gaze. "Her skin blistered and scarred so she started tattooing as a way to claim her skin back. If people were going to stare anyway, she decided to have them stare for good reason. This is the outward expression of her inner self, an alchemy of her physical curse and the archetypes within her mind. We are embodied souls, after all."

"What happens at the end?" Jamie asked, thinking of the implant of ashes they had seen upstairs. She pointed at Tem's heavily tattooed forearms. "When your body dies, is that the end of the meaning to the images?"

Tem looked serious. "In my culture, yes." He nodded. "The spirit lives on, but after death the body is buried, returned to *Papatuanuku*, Mother Earth." Tem paused for a moment. "But others revere the physical form. I've heard of specialists in skin preservation, those who work with the bodies of the dead to keep tats for family or gang affiliation. I've also heard rumors of a skin trade, a black market for inked skin. Fetishists mostly." He shook his head. "But after what I've put onto people's bodies, nothing surprises me these days."

Jamie thought of the missing and the dead so far. All were inked.

"Do you know where we could find someone like that in London?" she asked.

Tem shook his head. "Really not my thing. I prefer live bodies to work with, skin I have permission to ink." Tem pointed along the corridor. "Go see the taxidermists. They have their own little community." Tem looked at Jamie, meeting her eyes. "And come and see me when you make your decision about what you want inked."

Jamie blushed under his gaze, wondering what it would feel like to have his strong hands inking her skin. Part of her wanted to find out.

"Thanks for your help," Blake said, breaking the moment. He shook Tem's hand. "We really appreciate it."

They walked away from Tem's stand towards a corner of the convention hidden amongst the arches. Here were the cabinet-of-curiosity shops where strange objects were sold alongside herbal remedies, and taxidermists displayed their wares. The people who sat on the stalls generally wore black, many were tattooed, and Jamie wondered at the crossover between the groups. Was it a fascination with death or just with skin?

They walked around, trying to get a sense of who to speak to. One stall displayed beetles and spiders, butterflies and frogs pinned on boards, their remains spread out for viewing. The vibrant colors of the shiny carapaces and wetness of the skin made them look like they had recently been caught and mounted. Jamie was reminded of Damien Hirst's *Last Kingdom* piece, which placed dead insects in exact rows, a rainbow of colors of the dead. Was it all just *memento mori*, Jamie wondered, to help us remember that we are all animated dust waiting to return to the earth?

Blake wandered over to an area with pieces of furniture that had been modified to incorporate taxidermy animals. He bent to a red wingback chair to examine two young foxes, stuffed as if they were playing and mounted into the hollow back. Jamie turned to another stall nearby.

It had animal heads mounted on wooden bases, but they weren't in the style of hunting lodges where old men boasted of their kill. These heads were embellished with colorful beads and jeweled flowers, embroidered silk and ribbons. Each piece turned the animal into a celebration of life. Jamie stopped to look more closely and a young woman came out from behind the table. Her hair was ash blonde, tied back from her pale face with a garland of flowers. Her eyes were intelligent, slightly wary, as if she expected criticism for her work.

"Hi," she said, her voice timid. "Can I help you?"

"These are beautiful," Jamie said, and she found herself meaning it. The initial revulsion of these dead bodies had been replaced by fascination for the beauty of the objects.

"Thank you," the young woman said. "I mostly make custom taxidermy for collections and private museums, but my passion is turning the dead into flower gardens." She pointed at a deer's head. "And of course, no animals are ever killed for the purpose. I only use roadkill."

Jamie thought of this young woman walking along the edge of a quiet road in the countryside, waiting to stumble upon dead animals.

Blake wandered back over from the chairs to join the conversation.

"Can I ask what your fascination is with taxidermy?" he asked. His attention made the young woman bloom a little. Her eyes darted away from his handsome face and back again. *Must be tough to get a date when your house is full of dead animals*, Jamie thought.

"Ultimately, it's about respect for the animal and for life itself," the young woman said, her voice growing stronger as she talked. "You can get closer to it than you ever could in life. I study anatomy so I can get the dimensions right and make sure the muscle shapes are clear. And it's also art, creating something that will make people think. Perhaps it's the ultimate blend of science and art, chemistry and sculpture."

"Is there much of a community in London?" Blake asked.

The young woman nodded enthusiastically. "Oh yes, we have meetups and classes. It's quite a scene. The tattoo conventions mostly have a section for us as well, so we get to meet new people all the time."

"We're looking for someone," Jamie said. "He – or she – works with human tattooed skin, preserving it after death. Do you know of anyone like that?"

"There is a man …" The young woman hesitated, her eyes guarded. "He doesn't really advertise but I've been to his place once – a while ago. He might not be there anymore."

"We'd really like to try and track him down," Blake said. "Can you give us his address?"

"It's more of a squat than a residential place," she replied. "Out by Limehouse Cut."

Jamie pulled out her smartphone and opened a map application. The young woman showed her an approximate area.

***

As they walked out of the convention, Blake turned to Jamie.

"That place was not what I expected, but it makes me want to mark my skin." He touched his gloved hands together gently. "With something more than scars." He thought about the runes in the Galdrabók, how they would look on his caramel skin. Would inking them on his body help him to claim their power or perhaps even tame his curse? He looked at Jamie. "What about you?"

"When we came in here, I was still unsure. But now I have a clearer idea. I want birds on the wing." Jamie touched her neck on the right side. "Maybe here, down my shoulder onto my back."

"Escape? Freedom?" Blake said, thinking that tattoos on

Jamie's skin would also be damn sexy. "A desire to transcend this physical life, perhaps?"

Jamie grinned. "It's rude to ask the meaning of someone's tattoo."

"Even one that doesn't exist yet?"

They walked to Jamie's bike and she pulled a second helmet from her pannier. "Can you come?" she asked, offering it to him.

Blake hesitated. Every hour he was away from the museum was another nail in the coffin of his research career. He looked down into Jamie's hazel eyes and saw that she needed him. Her friend was missing and perhaps he could still help find her.

"Of course I'm coming," he said. "I work in the museum with a load of mummified remains. I can't miss out on meeting a real-life skin preserver."

CHAPTER 13

THIRTY MINUTES LATER, BLAKE shook his head as he pulled off the motorbike helmet, running his gloved fingers over his buzz cut.

"That is too much fun," he said, handing the helmet back to Jamie. "Even if I have to ride pillion."

"One of the pleasures of life," Jamie said. "Not really enough open road around London though."

She looked up at the sixties concrete block in front of them. It had been a technical college once, later abandoned and now inhabited by an eclectic group of artists, many of whom also lived in the building. Some might call them squatters but in this part of East London, turning a derelict building into something this productive was akin to a miracle. Rejuvenation of the old Docklands was happening slowly and the artists were often the first to move in.

"Nice place," Blake said with raised eyebrows as he stepped gingerly over a bare needle on the broken concrete path.

"Let's take a look inside," Jamie said.

She pushed open the front door to reveal a neglected corridor strewn with the detritus of people living rough. Cardboard boxes and string, a folded blanket and old tins of beans. It smelled of stale sweat and sweet marijuana smoke.

Music thumped through the building and they followed the noise along the corridor to the back of the structure. It had a deafening bass that Jamie recognized as "Closer" by Nine Inch Nails. A hymn to finding God in desecration and violation, a song to bring alive the crazy in anyone. A song she remembered playing as a teenager bent on escaping a mundane existence, desperate for something more than suburbia. Strange to hear it again here.

A metal door barred their way. Jamie rapped on it, but there was no chance that anyone would hear them inside with that racket. She pushed at the door but it was firmly locked from the inside. She hammered with her fist as the song came to an end, but no one came to let them in. The bass kicked in on the next song and their knocking was drowned out once more.

"Let's go round the outside," Jamie said, and they walked back out.

The building was on the edge of the Limehouse Cut, a waterway that ran from the River Lea down to the Thames. The sun sparkled on the slow-moving water, bringing a moment of beauty to this urban junkyard.

"Come look at this," Blake said, as he walked towards the side of the building. A ramshackle houseboat was tied up there, its moorings rusted and weed-covered from its long-term berth. He pointed at the name of the boat, the paint chipped and faded but still clearly visible.

"Pyx?" Jamie said. "I don't get it."

"It's one of the oldest doors in Westminster Abbey," Blake said. "Anglo-Saxon and over a thousand years old. What's more interesting is that it has panels of skin upon it that some believe were from the bodies of flayed criminals, left there as a warning to those who would attack the church."

They walked along the narrow path behind the building. Huge windows dominated the back section and a door stood open a little further on. A man stood on the back step blowing smoke rings into the air, his eyes closed in bliss as the bassline pumped from the studio behind him. He was tall and thin, his body held with the slumped posture of one who worked hunched over most of the time and often had to bend in the presence of others. His limbs were long and gangly, as if he had never had the nutrition to help him grow into them. His skin was pale, his head closely shaven and smooth, reflecting the sun.

His eyes flicked open at their approach and he quickly stubbed out the cigarette.

"Please wait," Jamie shouted, waving at him.

The man stepped inside the studio and Jamie ran to the open door, reaching it as he tried to force it closed. She wedged her foot into the crack.

"Please," she shouted above the music. "We only want to talk to you."

"I don't have anything here. No money, no drugs," the man pleaded, his face desperate as he tried to push Jamie out. Blake stood behind her.

"We're not here to take anything," he said. "We're looking for a friend and we heard you could help."

"I'm a private investigator on a missing persons case," Jamie added. "Please just talk with us for a second."

The man's features softened as he realized they weren't there to steal from him. Jamie could understand his anxiety in this part of town.

"Alright," he said, moving back from the door. "Let me turn the music off."

Jamie and Blake stood by the door as the music quietened and the man returned.

"Great album," Jamie said. "I always loved Trent Reznor."

"Forgive me, I don't get too many visitors in this part of town. Most are here looking to score." He took a deep breath. "I'm Corium Jones." The man's features softened and he held out a hand. The skin was red and raw with evident chemical burns but Jamie shook it without flinching, meeting his eyes as she did so.

"I'm Jamie Brooke and this is Blake Daniel."

"What can I help you with?" Corium asked.

"We were at the tattoo convention," Jamie said, "and heard that you provide an unusual service for those with body art."

Corium nodded, a wry smile on his lips.

"Yes, people pay me to preserve their tattoos after death," he said. "It's a growing industry. After all, they may have paid thousands to emblazon their skin with meaning in life and so they want to pass that on somehow. Their lifetime stories are inked into their skin, and they don't want it to rot away. They can't imagine the worms devouring it, or the fire consuming it. Skin preservation is an ancient art with few of us left. And, of course, much misunderstood."

"Can we have a look?" Jamie asked, glancing behind him into the dark of the studio.

Corium paused and Jamie felt the intensity of his gaze as he assessed her and Blake. Perhaps he sensed the death around them both, because after a moment, he stepped aside and waved them in.

The room had several workbenches with tools lined up neatly on one side. There was a vat of salt in one corner and a skin pegged out on a frame in the shade of an open window, the faint blue lines of a tattoo barely visible on the opposite side.

The smell of chemical preservative hung in the air, reminding Jamie of the studio of Rowan Day-Conti, the artist who had worked with the plastination of dead bodies. She shuddered when she remembered how the Jenna Neville case had ended for Rowan, trying to keep an open mind about what they might find here.

"How does your service actually work?" Jamie asked. "Do you cut from the bodies directly?"

Corium laughed. "I don't deal in bodies, only in skin. My clients pay for services, the skin arrives, usually rough cut in medical boxes. I prepare it, mount it as directed and then return it to the specified address. There's actually no personal contact – except with the skin, of course."

He stepped to a bench and indicated a piece of what looked like leather.

"This one is ready for mounting." He stroked the edge of it, his face showing pride in his work. "You can touch it if you like. It's very soft. Young skin, I think."

"So you don't actually know where the skin comes from?" Blake asked.

"Not at all," Corium said. "It's not my job to ask, either. I merely act as the preserver."

Jamie shook her head slowly. The man's words seemed logical in one way, and he was just a leather worker of a kind. But how could he touch these skins and not feel that they were once a thinking human?

"Can I ask what body parts you work on?" she asked.

Corium went to a row of shelves and pulled out one of the large photo albums stacked there. He laid it on the table and flicked it open.

"These are some of my favorite works," he said, a note of pride in his voice. He turned the first page. "These are the most common. Full-back tattoos which result in a rectangular finished piece, or two longer panels, depending on how close to the spine the skin was excised. There are also cross shapes where the shoulder and arm pieces have been saved."

Jamie swallowed her revulsion as she looked down at the pages, but the pictures were artistic, the skin turned into something beautiful. There was incredible skill in the ink and the colors: a waving riot of flowers that seemed to grow across the skin with blooming roses and curlicues in a feminine design.

A gigantic pair of strong angel wings, each feather inked

in detail, the size of the skin indicating it came from a large man.

A tiger prowling through a verdant jungle, its eyes staring out at the viewer.

There were quotes, too. In one, calligraphic handwriting flowed across the skin: *I'm the hero of this story. I don't need to be saved.* It seemed terribly sad that the hero was no more.

"Then there are the full-sleeve tattoos which result in a long tapering shape," Corium continued. "Very pleasing to the eye."

He indicated a lion's head in profile, its mane rippling over what had been muscles in life. A school of hammerhead sharks swimming over a submerged ancient city.

A list of coordinates with passport pictures and snapshots of faraway places.

A kaleidoscope of galaxies and stars in hues of cobalt blue, luminous greens and pinks.

The variation was incredible and Jamie could see how preserving these works of art was as much of a skill as inking them.

"I also have a number of head tattoos, which are more or less oval in shape, although it can be hard to get the edges right on those. They're the main ones," Corium raised his eyebrows, "but now and then I get some more intimate parts. Quite unusual, I must say."

Jamie looked at the shelf of photo albums.

"How long have you been doing this?" she asked.

"Since I was a child," Corium said, and the look in his eyes spoke of the deep loneliness of the misfit. "It started with taxidermy of small animals and tanning of found hides, but then one day a dying friend asked me to help preserve a part of himself and I couldn't say no. My reputation spread in the tattoo community and here in London these days there's no shortage of preservation work. There are also people who are willing to pay a lot of money for human leather products, from unmarked and inked skin."

Corium ran a hand across his smooth head. "I want ink myself of course, but I suffer from the tyranny of choice. After all, I have all these examples of fine art and I can't decide what I want on my own canvas. We have such a small amount of space and to get it wrong would be …" He shook his head and sighed. "Well, I can't abide the thought that my own legacy would be inferior to the skins I work on all day."

While Corium spoke, Jamie could see that Blake had wandered down to the far end of the studio to a tall book-case. He bent more closely to look at the books, and then turned to call back to them.

"Could you tell us about this particular book?"

Corium's head snapped round and his eyes narrowed. He had the look of a man who would protect his domain at any cost.

"It's an early edition of Francis Galton's *Hereditary Genius*. For a very private client." His voice was cold as he stalked down the studio, Jamie following close behind.

The shelves were mostly filled with photography books of tattoos and body art, with others on taxidermy and skin preservation. But one shelf had a thin book bound in soft leather. The pattern inked on the skin looked like dragon scales in hues of purple.

"Is it bound in human skin?" Blake asked.

"Anthropomorphic bibliopegy is a great tradition," Corium said. "Anatomy texts bound in the skin of cadavers, judicial proceedings bound in the skin of murderers –"

"Lampshades made from the skin of murdered Jews …" Blake whispered, looking more closely at the books. "Where do you draw the line?" He turned back to look at them and Jamie saw his blue eyes were steel-hard. "May I touch them?"

It wasn't a question. Corium nodded slowly. Blake removed one of his gloves and reached out to touch the book.

CHAPTER 14

BLAKE COULD SENSE VIBRATIONS on the surface of the skin through his fingertips, as if it held within itself the energy from the dead soul it had once bound in flesh. The veil of consciousness clouded his vision and he dipped into memory.

He found himself in a basement with high ceilings, the walls and floor tiled so they could be more easily hosed down. There was a copper smell in the cool air, the bitterness of blood. Empty meat hooks hung in a line on a railing above. There was an animal shriek in the darkness, a sound of terror that echoed through the empty space. Blake shuddered and tried to move, but the body he could see through was chained to the wall and couldn't escape.

He heard footsteps coming towards him and a whimper of fear echoed in the basement. He wanted to pull out of the trance, but he needed to see who was there. A man came out of the darkness, a skinning knife in his hand, his face obscured by the mask of the plague doctor, hooked beak swaying as he approached.

As panic escalated, Blake pulled himself from the trance, ripping his hand away from the book and collapsing to the floor. His breath came fast, his chest heaving as he tried to calm himself.

"It's OK, Blake," Jamie whispered, stroking his forehead. "You're safe now."

She gave him some water and he sipped at it, slowly recovering his breath. Corium Jones stood looking at them, his eyes narrowed in interest but not judgement or doubt. Blake supposed that the man was used to the odd in his line of work. But how much did he know of the provenance of the skin he worked on?

"The skin was taken," Blake said after a moment. "This person was murdered for it but the man who did it hid his face. He wore one of those Venetian plague doctor masks with the long beak for herbs to prevent the smell and decay from reaching them."

"Do you have some kind of psychic ability?" Corium asked, fascination in his voice.

Blake stood up and put his glove back on.

"You could call it that," he said. "I can read the emotional resonance of objects."

Jamie pointed at the book. "Who gave you this skin?" she asked, her voice soft but insistent.

"I can't possibly divulge information about my clients," Corium said, turning to walk away from them towards the door. "I think it's time for you to leave now."

Blake took a quick step forward, his blue eyes blazing with anger.

"Don't you understand? This skin is from a murder victim."

"You have no evidence of that," Corium said, pulling open the door.

Jamie picked up a vial of chemicals from a bench next to the bookcase. She put the book of human skin next to it.

"What does this do?" she asked, waving the bottle. Corium's face fell as she pulled the stopper out and held it over the book.

Corium put his hands up in a gesture of supplication.

"No, please. That will burn the skin. It will ruin the book."

There was fear in his eyes, whether for the object itself or the person he made it for, Jamie didn't know. She tipped the bottle a little, splashing the bench next to the book. It made a sizzling sound and the smell of bitter berries filled the air.

"No!" Corium shouted, rushing across the room. Blake stepped in front of Jamie and pushed the man back, a rough shove in the middle of his thin chest.

"Tell us who the client is," Jamie said, holding the bottle over the book again.

Corium's body drooped, his shoulders slumping in defeat.

"I'll give you what I know," he said. "But it's not much." He walked to a filing cabinet in the corner and pulled out a thin cardboard file. "Here, that's everything. Now please, leave the book alone."

Blake checked the file quickly and nodded to Jamie. She put the stopper back in the bottle and put it down next to the book on the bench. Corium rushed to it, cradling the book to his chest like a precious child as he sank to the floor, sitting with his back to the bench as he watched them with hollow eyes.

Jamie pulled out the pages in the file. "There are regular payments here," she said with surprise. "How many of these have you done?"

"Six so far," Corium whispered. "But it's an ongoing contract. I'm expecting more skin in the next day or so and then I produce a book within the following month."

"There's barely any useful information here," she said. "Just a PO Box for the return address."

Blake pointed to the bottom of the page. "But the book is overdue for delivery, so maybe we can stake out the pickup?"

They turned back to Corium.

"Package it up," Jamie said. "We'll deliver it for you."

He clutched it to his chest.

"You don't understand," he said softly. "This is not a man you want to meet in person. He's not someone I want to cross, either. Please, don't do this."

Jamie walked over to him. "A friend of ours is missing," she said. "I don't want to see her skin on your bench." She held out her hands for the book. "If you won't package it, then I will. But we're taking the book."

Corium clutched it tighter. "He'll know if the package is done incorrectly," he whispered, his eyes darting around the room. "If you must take it, I'll do it for you."

He stood and placed the book gently on the bench, preparing the package and wrapping it in bubble wrap, then brown paper. A normal-looking parcel hiding a macabre object inside.

"There." He handed it to Jamie, his voice cold. "Now, get out."

"Gladly," Blake said, as they walked to the door and back out into the sunlight. Corium slammed the door behind them as they headed back along the Cut. Jamie held the package carefully in both hands.

"Did you get any sense of the person when you read?" she asked.

Blake shook his head. "Only the sheer terror of being chained up in what looked like an old abattoir – and the knowledge that the end was coming." He sighed. "I've felt that before. It's anticipation of the inevitable, but of course, those I read have not gone quietly or at peace."

"I'm sorry I involved you in this."

Blake reached out and pulled her to him. They stood for a moment in the sunlight, Blake's arms wrapped around her. Jamie relaxed into him, relishing the moment of connection.

"I'm not sorry," he said. "I want to help you, Jamie. And now I want to help O, too. The research I do at the museum doesn't change anything, but with you, I have the chance to make an impact on the living." He pulled away a little, looking down at her. "Now, let's go catch this crazy skin collector."

Jamie laughed and the moment lifted her spirits. She had begun to despair of finding O, but now they had a real lead. She wanted to call Missinghall and involve the police, but she knew that Blake's vision was inadmissible as evidence. Even if they raided Corium Jones' place, she now had the book of skin. It would take days to test and they would lose the chance to catch the collector when it was delivered.

"Do you know what Corium means?" Blake asked, checking his phone as they headed back towards the bike.

Jamie shook her head. "I just thought it was an unusual name."

"It's the Latin for dermis, one of the skin layers and also a term used for the thickened leathery part of an insect wing."

Jamie sighed, shaking her head. "Only in London," she said.

***

An hour later, Jamie walked into a post office delivery center further east in Plaistow and dropped the package off with a bored clerk on the front desk. He typed the information into his computer and gave Jamie a delivery receipt. As she turned to walk out of the office, he picked up the phone but Jamie couldn't hear his words. She walked back outside to find Blake standing by a lamppost opposite with two take-away coffees.

"Tell me that you have some kind of useful tracking mechanism," he said. "You've stuck a sticker on the package and we can track it with our phones, right?"

"Of course, my private investigator budget stretches to all kinds of Bond-style gadgets," Jamie said with a grin. "But since we're here, we might as well stake the place out. I think the clerk made a phone call about the package, so we might not be waiting too long." She took a sip of the coffee and looked at her watch. "I'm worried about it being another night before we find O. Corium's workshop looked exactly like the type of place some sick bastard would send her perfect skin to be turned into a book. Did you see anything else in the vision that might help us?"

"Only the abattoir setting," Blake said, pulling out his phone. He opened a map of the area. "Meat processing is mainly done outside the city these days, but an older map might help us with where the abattoirs once stood." He was silent for a moment and then showed Jamie the phone. "Look how close we are to the East London Crematorium," he said. "If you had to dispose of body parts, this would be a good place to do it."

"We could split up," Jamie said. "You can stay here and watch for anyone collecting the package and I'll go to the crematorium and see what I can find."

Blake raised an eyebrow. "Seriously? You want to go alone to the crematorium?"

Jamie shrugged. "The dead don't bother me. It's the living I worry about."

The buzz of a motorbike grew louder as it came up the hill and then pulled to a stop outside the post office. It was a courier bike with the logo of a well-known firm on the side. The leather-clad figure dismounted and then entered the delivery office.

"This must be it," Jamie said. She pulled on her helmet and sat astride the bike. "You coming?"

Blake grinned. "You really know how to give a boy a good time."

He pulled her spare helmet over his head, sitting behind her and wrapping his arms around her waist. The delivery man emerged with the brown paper package under his arm. He put it in one of the side panniers and headed off down the road. Jamie pulled out behind him, keeping him in sight as they drove further east.

The shops changed into housing estates, evidence of homelessness and job seekers in the rundown yards and people hanging out on the corners. Jamie stayed well back, but with the volume of traffic even this far out, it was unlikely the courier would be suspicious. He was only doing his job.

It wasn't long before the courier turned into an industrial estate with only one road in and out. Jamie pulled over at the edge of the road and watched as the bike turned out of sight around a corner towards what looked like a derelict warehouse. The courier opened a roller door, put the package inside, pulled the door back down, and then drove back out of the park. He glanced at Jamie and Blake as he turned from the estate, but with the nonchalance of live-and-let-live London, where anything goes.

As the courier roared away up the street, Jamie drove down to the warehouse, turning off the bike's engine outside the roller-door. Blake dismounted and pulled his helmet off and Jamie followed suit, pulling a flashlight from her pannier.

They stood for a moment, listening for any sound. All they could hear was the noise of the city. There was nothing from inside the building.

Blake reached down and pulled up the roller door to reveal an empty loading bay. The package sat inside the entrance.

"Leave it," Jamie whispered as Blake reached for it. Her years of working for the police had honed a sense of when something wasn't quite right and this place made her skin crawl.

There was a door at the back of the loading bay. Jamie pointed at it and Blake nodded. Together, they walked quietly towards it.

CHAPTER 15

THE DOOR WAS DOUBLE padlocked, but that didn't deter Blake.

"Misspent youth," he explained as he picked up a short metal pipe, swinging it a little to heft its weight. Wielding it like a hammer, it only took a few sharp blows to smash off the padlocks. The sound of the metal clashing resounded in the loading bay, and it would definitely warn anyone inside of their presence.

The door opened silently at Jamie's push, evidence that it had been oiled recently which seemed out of place in a derelict building. It was dark inside, but she could sense a wide space in front of them and the sharp lines of machinery loomed from the shadows. A metallic smell pervaded the air. As Blake stepped in behind Jamie, he grasped the door frame, his knuckles white with tension.

"This has to be the place," he whispered. "I recognize the smell of old blood."

As her eyes adjusted to the darkness, Jamie realized the machinery was for meat processing and packaging. Chains and hooks, winches used for heavy carcasses, blades for cutting, crushing weights. She shivered a little, imagining the place spattered in the blood of dead animals. She turned on the flashlight quickly and the beam reflected off shiny surfaces within. The equipment was spotless and left pristine, although a thin layer of dust had settled over it, evidence of time passing since the last animal was processed here.

"This isn't the slaughter room," Blake whispered. "We need to go deeper into the factory."

If she had still been in the police, it would have been well past the time to call for backup, but Jamie knew they wouldn't come for an empty, disused abattoir with a bad feeling about it. Her rational side understood the craziness of following a hunch based on Blake's psychic vision, but he had been right before and they had no other leads on finding O.

She shone the torch around the large processing area, finally locating a door behind one of the machines.

"That way," she said, walking with light feet across the warehouse, her senses alert for any sound. It was so quiet here, too quiet. Blake's hand found hers and squeezed gently as they crossed the space.

"We'll find her," he said, but his voice was shaky.

What had he seen in the vision that had affected him so much? Jamie wondered. And would they face it again in reality behind this door?

There were signs next to the door indicating a cold zone and the safety equipment necessary to enter the slaughter-house rooms. Jamie pushed the handle down and the door swung open.

She shone the beam inside with her arm outstretched, panning it around the long room. The floor and walls were tiled and meat hooks hung down on chains from the ceiling. A long metal table stood in the middle with grooves down the sides and a drain underneath. Jamie couldn't help but imagine the table running with blood, crimson circling the drain as life ebbed away.

A dripping sound echoed through the space.

"That's water from a cooling system," Jamie said. "If the place is deserted, it shouldn't be on."

She stepped into the room and walked past the table heading for the shadows at the far end. Blake followed close behind, his breath coming fast. The silence was oppressive, as if the walls of the building were closing in on them, ready to crush them into pieces. Jamie couldn't stand the quiet any longer.

"Olivia," she called, her voice echoing in the chamber. "Is anyone here?"

As the echoes died away, they waited in silence but no noise came back except the dripping of water. They walked to the back of the space and found two enormous fridge doors. There was a low buzzing noise, evidence that the fridges were running.

Blake pulled at one of the doors and it swung open, an automatic light coming on inside.

"Oh no," he whispered as he saw what was within.

"What is it?" Jamie yanked the handle, pulling the door fully open so she could see inside.

A metal table sat against one side of the fridge. On top of it were several pieces of flesh, each covered in a tattoo. There were two long strips, one tattooed with a rainbow that Jamie recognized from the picture of Nicholas Randolph. She pushed down the nausea that rose within her. She had been at so many crime scenes, but there was something macabre about this one. The pieces of flesh were clinically clean. But for the tattoos, they wouldn't have known this had once been a man.

"I have to call it in," Jamie said. "This is a police matter now."

"What about the other fridge?" Blake gestured towards the other door, his face sickly pale in the harsh light. Jamie gulped down her hesitation and yanked it open, ready to face whatever horrors might be within.

As the automatic light flickered on, Jamie saw the thin figure huddled in the corner, arms wrapped around herself, head drooped to one side, features pale with a blueish tinge.

Jamie rushed inside and pulled O into her arms, feeling for the pulse at her neck. There was a faint beat there, but it was slow and unsteady. Blake blocked the fridge door open and together they carried O's unconscious form out into the main slaughter area. Blake pulled off his jacket and wrapped it around O's body and head, pulling her close to his warm frame as he rubbed her arms.

Jamie pulled out her phone and called for an ambulance and the police.

***

Several hours later, Jamie and Blake sat in the Royal London Hospital emergency waiting room. They had given detailed statements to the officers in charge of the scene, and after Jamie had spoken to Missinghall, they'd been allowed to leave.

Jamie tapped her foot on the floor, a rhythmic sound of impatience.

"They'll tell us when she's awake," Blake said, putting his hand on her arm. "There's nothing more we can do."

"I hope she remembers the bastard who took her." Jamie stood up and paced the floor. "Missinghall said the abattoir was clean. No prints. Just a lot of bleach. Whoever it was knew police procedure."

A nurse poked her head around the doorway.

"Olivia's awake. She wants to see you, Ms Brooke."

Jamie looked over at Blake and he nodded his head.

"It's OK, I'll stay here and wait for you. She doesn't even know me."

"I'll make sure she understands about your part in finding her," Jamie said. She followed the nurse out of the room and down a white corridor to the ward area. The smell of antiseptic reminded Jamie too much of the morgues she had frequented as part of the homicide team. It was a smell that masked disease and decay in her mind, not a scent of health and wellness. The nurse pointed out a tiny room where a police officer stood outside the door.

"Ten minutes," she warned. "Then she has to rest."

Jamie gave her name to the officer, and after he had checked her ID, she stepped inside. O lay curled up in the bed, wrapped in warming blankets around her body and over her head in a hood. Her eyes were bright blue against her ice-pale skin, but her lips had a pinkish hue now. She would make it.

"How you doing?" Jamie asked, sitting by the bed.

"Better than earlier," O whispered, her voice hoarse. "Thank you."

The words were simple, but Jamie understood the edge of death. She had come close to it herself in the Hellfire Caves and she knew what it meant to come back from the brink.

"Do you know who it was?" she asked.

O shut her eyes for a moment and then sighed. "I wish I did. I was walking back to the flat late last night. I'm not afraid to walk in Southwark – it's my patch, you know." Jamie nodded for O to continue. "As I walked under the arches at London Bridge, a figure came up behind me and covered my mouth with a cloth, holding me tight, and then it was only blackness. The next thing I knew I was shivering in that fridge." She fell silent for a moment. "But I heard a knife being sharpened, Jamie. That metallic repetition as the blade is drawn over and over on the lodestone … and later I heard screaming."

"I believe you," Jamie said. "There were – packages – in the fridge next to yours, but no fingerprints or anything in trace evidence to help us find whoever did it."

"He came in once," O said, her voice so quiet that Jamie had to lean in closer. "He wore black clothes and a floor-length black apron, and a mask on his face with a long beak."

"The Venetian plague doctor?" Jamie asked.

O nodded. "Yes, I've seen similar ones. The mask gave me hope because if he didn't want me to see his face, then he was going to let me go. But then he told me to strip. It was so cold, but I did what he asked. He told me to spin around and show him the extent of the octopus tattoo. I couldn't see his eyes but I felt them on my body. It was like he was measuring me up for something. It was the first time I've wanted to scrub the ink from my skin." Tears glistened in O's eyes and one rolled down her cheek to the pillow. Jamie reached forward and took her hand, waiting for her to carry on. "As I turned, he said that it was a shame I wouldn't be dancing at the masquerade ball. Then he told me to dress and that he would be back."

"And then?" Jamie asked.

"Then I tried to stay warm … and then you were there."

There were voices outside the room and then the door burst open. Magda rushed in, her face stricken, arms outstretched. Jamie stood and let her take her place by O's side, the tears of both women mingling on the pillow as they whispered to each other.

Jamie walked to the window, looking out as they talked for a moment in low voices. She remembered waking up in hospital after the Hellfire Caves, how Blake had been by her side, his hand near hers on the bed. A flicker of a smile played on her lips. It made all the difference having someone who cared enough to be there. She thought of him waiting for her a corridor away. They were both such damaged people, but perhaps there was hope that together, they could transcend their history.

"Thank you, Jamie," Magda said. "If you hadn't found her when you did …"

"I don't think this is the end of it," Jamie said. "We didn't find the man responsible, and if O's right, he could be targeting the masquerade ball next."

"So many of the people going have ink," O said. "Lots of my friends from Torture Garden are attending. Any excuse to dress up extravagantly."

"I need to call my contact at the police and let him know about the threat," Jamie said. "Is there anything else you need?"

O smiled and squeezed Magda's hand. "I've got everything I need right here."

Jamie left them together and emerged back into the corridor. She called Missinghall and he answered quickly.

"Damn it, Jamie," he said. "Those tattooed body parts reminded me of those specimens from the Hunterian case last year. You always seem to find the weirdest crime scenes."

"It started out as a missing persons case, Al. Things just got a little crazy."

"Well, it's definitely got the notice of the big guns around here. Dale Cameron is heading up the case himself now, taking a personal interest in the murders and also pursuing the tattoo angle. He sent a handpicked team to the abattoir. You know he's running for Mayor, right?"

"You mentioned it," Jamie said. "So I guess he's heavily invested in finding whoever's involved."

"Exactly," Missinghall said. "His slogan is 'clean up the city,' so he's trying to make sure that starts now."

"There might be more trouble coming," Jamie said. "I've spoken with Olivia, and she told me that the man who abducted her mentioned the Southbank masquerade ball."

"That's tomorrow night at the Tate Modern," Missinghall said. "We can't shut it down at this stage, but it will be full of the city's finest, including the Mayoral candidates. Let me get the information to the security team and I'm sure they'll assign more security. We'll get this bastard, Jamie."

CHAPTER 16

LEAVING O IN MAGDA'S care, Jamie walked back along the corridor into the waiting room. Blake stood as she entered.

"How is she?" he asked.

"Alive – and grateful." Jamie smiled and for a moment it seemed as if everything was right with the world. She walked into Blake's arms and hugged him, her arms wrapped around his strong back, the warmth of his body against hers. She inhaled his masculine scent and they stood together, just breathing. The seconds ticked past and what had started as a friendly hug between friends morphed into the edge of something more intimate.

Jamie's heart beat faster as she felt an overwhelming desire to lift her mouth for his kiss. He was a beautiful man, and his scars and wounded soul only made him more desirable. She wondered what his bare hands would feel like on her skin. Would he be able to read the desire from her body as he read objects? She took a deep breath. This couldn't happen, not now. Perhaps not ever.

She stepped back, exhaling slowly. Blake's eyes were cobalt blue and she saw her own desire reflected there.

"I need to go," she said, too aware of his proximity. "It's late."

Blake nodded. "It's been a long day."

They walked together out of the hospital, the silence between them no longer comfortable but heavy with unsaid words. When they reached Jamie's bike, Blake refused the pillion helmet.

"I'll get the Tube back," he said. "I know you prefer to ride alone."

Jamie couldn't tell him how much she had relished his arms around her waist as they had zoomed around London together. How his heat against her back had made her feel again. How she longed for more.

She put her helmet on, needing its protective shield to stop her words from escaping.

"Thank you for coming today," she said. "You're the one who really found O."

"We did it together," Blake said. "We make a good team." He reached for her hand and squeezed it. "Sleep well, Jamie."

He turned to leave, but she called him back.

"I'm … going to go to the masquerade ball tomorrow night," she said, her words hesitant. "O told me that the man mentioned it, so perhaps he'll be there. I need to find him, Blake, and Southwark won't sleep easy until he's caught."

The corner of Blake's mouth twitched in a slight smile. "So it's more of a stakeout then," he said. "Definitely not a date."

"Definitely not," Jamie said, but she couldn't help but smile back.

Blake nodded. "I'd better sort out a costume then. I'll look forward to seeing you tomorrow."

As he walked away through the car park, Jamie roared off on her bike, back through East London towards the south. As she rode, she felt the crazy rise inside her. When she felt like this, she needed speed and escape.

She wanted to drink and dance, to stamp her claim on life and shout to the world that she was alive.

Finding O felt like a chink of light in the darkness, a triumph that she needed to celebrate. Life was so short and dark men could cut it shorter still. Or illnesses like the one that had taken her daughter from her. Death is inevitable, the only question is when and what can be done with this life as the seconds tick away. While blood still pumped in her veins, Jamie felt the need to snatch these moments of pleasure and revel in them.

She rode back to her flat, grabbed her tango bag, and headed back out into the night.

The tango *milonga* was a place of transformation. No one questioned anyone's identity outside, because only the dance mattered in here. It was the early hours of the morning now so only the hardcore remained, those with the stamina to dance for so long, those with the addiction to movement.

Sebastian was there, dancing with a young woman whose body seemed molded to his. He saw Jamie come in and nodded at her. He was always the one she wanted, the chemistry when they danced together was as close to sex as she could get without taking her clothes off.

Jamie put her tall heels on, letting her hair out of the clasp so it fell in dark waves down her back. She shook it out and stepped to the edge of the dance floor as the music faded and Sebastian left his partner to come to her.

There was no need to speak. Their bodies were all the conversation necessary and as the bandoneon began to play, Jamie surrendered to the movement. This was the loss of control she craved. The male role was dominant in tango, he led and she followed, bending to his touch and spinning at the pressure of his fingers on her flesh.

Sebastian had the perfect arrogance necessary in a tango partner, but with an edge of tragedy that filled every step with meaning. Jamie sublimated her desire into the steps, arching into him. She looked up into his eyes as he held her in close embrace, bending her backwards and pressing himself down upon her. She sensed that he would take this further if she gave assent. But dancing with Sebastian would change if they took it any further.

The pleasure of tango was in frustrated desire held in check, not the release. The fantasy of how it might feel to be possessed by him was more erotic than the taking would surely be. But Jamie was glad of the spark, glad that she was not defined only by the loss of her daughter or her work. As a dancer, she was a desirable woman, and the darkness she faced outside didn't matter right now. Here was only life.

CHAPTER 17

THE FIGURE WITH THE skinning knife took another step towards him, bending over his prone form. The blade flashed as it caught the light and then it descended, cutting into his flesh. The touch was gentle at first, a caress along his chest followed by a bead of dark blood. But then the pain began as the man pressed the knife deeper.

Blake twisted, trying to get away from the blade, but he was trapped, tied down, unable to move. His breath came in ragged gasps.

The man laughed and Blake saw the scar that marred his nose, the craggy features of the man he had seen in the museum.

He woke with a start, pulling himself out of the twisted bedclothes. He sat up and deliberately calmed his breathing as the sounds of London waking came from the window. The light was dull, grey clouds scudded past and the wind whistled through the chimney pots in the roof above. Blake took a deep breath. These were the sounds of his flat. He was safe.

He reached for the silver hip flask next to his bed, his hand hovering over it for a second. *Just a little*, he thought, taking a quick swig. Tequila was better for dulling the visions, but this early in the morning and before work, vodka was a better choice.

Feeling calmer now, Blake turned and sat on the edge of the bed, reaching underneath it for the package wrapped in dirty ivory sailcloth. His bare fingertips brushed it and Blake pulled away, reaching instead for the gloves by his bedside. This was a book he dared not read again with bare hands, since the visions had been so bloody and violent on the day his father had died.

Blake pulled the gloves on and then reached back under the bed, pulling out the tightly wrapped book. The Galdrabók. His father had used rites from the grimoire to summon powers of persuasion and charisma to lead his extremist Christian sect. In the last moments of his life, Blake had seen him consumed by demons come to claim what he had bargained for earthly power.

Or at least he had seen a vision through his father's eyes of what he'd *believed* was there to claim him. The visions were so tightly bound to the people he saw through, Blake was never sure how much could be considered objectively real. He smiled, shaking his head. Could demons ever be considered truth?

He pulled open the sailcloth to reveal the Galdrabók, its cover of deep burgundy leather inscribed with a circle bisected by four lines ending in prongs. Each line was cross-hatched with other markings, each a form of controlled chaos, like a deformed snowflake that had missed its natural perfection.

Blake opened the book, gazing again at the pages of Icelandic spells, invocations to demons and Christian saints. There were symbols and images for calling on the Norse gods and instructions on how to use herbs for visions of the otherworld. There were runes and symbols of power, Icelandic magic sigils, Latin texts and sacred images within. It was a dense bible of pagan belief, but Blake didn't really know what to make of it.

The museum researcher part of him wanted to take it

in for study, to academically discern the meaning of the symbols and words within. The book could be a lifetime of research, perhaps a way for him to discover the Nordic half of his family tree and give his academic life some deeper meaning. His mind skipped forward to conferences in the icy north, tweed jackets with elbow patches, book signings with bearded colleagues.

But the other part of him, perhaps the Nigerian half from his mother, perhaps the part that allowed him to see visions through time – that part wanted to read the book with bare hands laid upon it and speak the words within. His mind flashed to the vision of the ash grove, the human sacrifices to Odin, the power that hummed through those present. There was a world a long way from London, up in the dark forests of the Arctic Circle.

Blake closed the book and traced the symbol on the front with gloved fingertips. He thought of the man he had seen in the museum, the man who now haunted his dreams. Had the book really belonged to his father, or had he stolen it? Blake placed his hand flat on the burgundy leather. Was the stranger here to take it back?

***

An hour later, Blake walked up the steps into the British Museum, his close-cropped hair still wet from the shower. The Galdrabók was tucked safely beneath his bed again, the decision on what to do with it put off for now. Blake felt spring fever in the air, a sense that something was changing, and if he didn't move with it, he would be left behind.

He walked into the Great Court, looking up at the glass panels above, the sun streaming through. He descended to the research area and waved at Margaret in her office as he sat at his desk to work on some of the text for the exhibit. To his consternation, she stood and walked towards him.

"Morning," Blake said, his voice jolly as she approached.

"You weren't here much yesterday," Margaret said. No small talk today. "Even after our discussion."

"I was actually researching the sex trade in Southwark," Blake said. "To add some color to the exhibition."

Margaret raised an eyebrow. "Interesting. Well, your research might come in handy, as the curator needs a hand constructing the exhibition space. I'm volunteering you for the job since you can't seem to sit still down here."

"But –" Blake protested, but Margaret held a hand up.

"I actually think you'll enjoy it," she said with a smile.

Blake walked back upstairs towards the exhibition space, right in the middle of the Great Court. There was a security guard on the door to keep out the tourists. Blake showed his pass and then went into the central space. The walls were black and could be shifted around to bisect the space into various sizes, all the better to display the objects within. Spotlights lit the glass cases and Blake could see that the curator was aiming to entertain as well as educate.

The first case contained an array of phalluses – from the stone carvings offered to the gods for fertility, to the wind chimes of winged penises from first-century Roman London used to ward away evil spirits. It was a comical display, setting the tone for a tongue-in-cheek ride through erotic London.

A clanging noise came from further in.

Blake followed the sound into a larger space, where a petite blonde woman struggled to maneuver a leather stool onto a stage area. Her long hair was tied back in a simple ponytail and her plain blue jeans and black t-shirt gave her the air of a graduate student.

"Let me help with that," Blake said, helping her to lift the stool up. Once in place, he ran his gloved hand over the metal rivets at the edges. "Well made, isn't it."

"Yes," the woman said, a cheeky smile on her face. "Britain makes some of the best spanking stools and bondage gear."

Blake pulled his hand away quickly and the woman laughed.

"I'm Catherine Agew," she said.

"You're the guest curator for the exhibition," Blake said. He had assumed that the curator would be older … and not so good-looking.

"You must be Blake. Margaret said she was sending someone up to help me with the lifting and shifting."

Blake raised an eyebrow. "Lifter and shifter at your service." He turned to look at the stage area. "So what's this going to be?"

"Flagellation was a popular sexual service, especially in Georgian London and particularly amongst the nobility," Catherine said. "Brits have always enjoyed a good spanking."

She pointed at a wall filled with images of Victorian pornography, some of the more acceptable pictures from the museum's extensive collection. A black and white illustration showed a bewigged aristocrat bent over by a window, a woman beating his behind with birch twigs.

Blake found his eyes lingering on one image where a young woman lay over the knees of an older man, her blonde hair hanging down as he raised his hand to spank her. He turned away to find Catherine looking at him, curiosity in her eyes. He swallowed. Suddenly it seemed stuffy in here.

"So," he said. "What do you need me to do here?"

Catherine smiled and pointed out some of the other items to be placed on the stage, creating a tableau of a boudoir in one of the high-end establishments. Blake began to move the furniture, trying to push the lewd images from his mind.

Catherine's fingers lingered on his arm as he moved the final piece into position and Blake understood the possibility implied there. Before he had met Jamie, he had been living well in the promiscuous London singles scene, fueled by alcohol and a desire to forget. He had never had any trouble finding willing partners, but he struggled to take anything further than a one-night stand. Questions about his scars and doubts about his own demons had stopped him. But Jamie had given him hope that he could give more of himself, and tonight he would see her at the masquerade ball. Perhaps tonight they would be more than friends.

He took a step back, away from Catherine's touch.

"It looks great," he said. "I like that you've added humor to what could be a – difficult – exhibition."

"I'm glad you think so, but I also wanted to portray the darker side," Catherine said. "Whores who got on the wrong side of the law were sent to Bridewell house of correction and whipped in public. There were many who enjoyed watching and who paid for the privilege. Who were the real sinners after all?"

Catherine's eyes hardened and even with her small stature, Blake could see how much this exhibition meant to her.

"It's good that you're the curator," he said. "It's almost a feminist take on the sex trade, something that many wouldn't have considered."

Catherine's face softened and she sighed.

"Thank you. It means a lot to me to reclaim some of the myths. Of course the sex trade had its horrific side, but there were also women who made a lot of money with it. If they didn't die of disease or violence, they could live more independently than ever. Profits from the sex industry actually financed the development of huge swathes of the city. It was one of the most valuable commercial activities in the eighteenth and early nineteenth century, as important as even the London Docks."

Blake shook his head. "It's one of the paradoxes of London. Some of its greatest achievements come from the shadow side."

"Of course, it's difficult to know where to draw the line," Catherine said, the cheeky smile returning to her face. "The truth of London's past is often hidden for good reason." She pulled out some old street signs. "I want to put a couple of these up around the exhibit. What do you think?"

She shuffled through them so Blake could read the texts: Maiden Lane, Love Lane, Codpiece Lane, Gropecunt Lane. He put a hand up to stop her, laughing a little.

"I think that last one would bring in a raft of complaints," he said.

"It became Grape Street and then Grub Street over time," Catherine said. "But I quite like the original name. At least you knew what you were going to get there."

They worked with an easy camaraderie for the rest of the afternoon, the exhibition taking shape around them. Blake enjoyed watching Catherine work, her strong sense of what she wanted to portray commanding the space. Flirtation aside, she inspired him with the way she could use an exhibit to make people laugh and think, to make them feel. He understood why Margaret wanted him up here. He was reminded once more what a future in the museum might mean, what he could do with his gifts. He could bring the past alive and the thought enlivened him.

Blake looked at his watch. He still needed to pick up the tuxedo from the rental shop before heading to the Tate Modern for the ball.

"I've got to run," Blake said. "But I can help you tomorrow if you like?"

"I'll look forward to it," Catherine said with a smile that promised far more.

Blake emerged from the central exhibition space into the crowded Great Court. Tourists and families thronged the space and the noise of the crowd rose in waves. A lone figure caught Blake's eye. The man with the scar on his nose stood by the door of the Enlightenment Room, his piercing blue eyes fixed on Blake.

Blake's heart thudded in his chest as he recognized aspects of his father in the man's face, and the promise of the north in his eyes.

He took a step forward.

The man ducked into the Enlightenment Room behind him. Blake followed, expecting to find him there, wanting to challenge him. The room swirled with people, but the man was gone. For now, at least.

CHAPTER 18

THE VAST EXPANSE OF the Turbine Hall at the Tate Modern was transformed for the masquerade ball.

High ceilings were crisscrossed with thin wires at one end and acrobats walked with long poles over the crowd. Trapeze artists swung across the expanse, tumbling across the space to be caught before the long drop to the concrete floor. Long silk ribbons hung down in another area and four lithe women wound themselves up before letting themselves spin towards the ground, plunging in barely controlled descent. The acrobats wore close-fitting, almost see-through body suits with artfully placed embroidery and crystals reflecting the light. Their limbs were etched against the black roof, the embodied perfection of human art in this temple to creation.

Jamie stood for a moment, looking up in wonder at the kaleidoscope of color and movement above. The sounds of a live jazz band accompanied the performers, although the dancing would start in earnest as the alcohol flowed more freely. Jamie remembered the night she had taken Polly to Cirque du Soleil, a circus that celebrates the extremes of the human body, communicating story through movement and music. Polly's body had been ravaged by motor neuron disease by then, but her eyes had been alive with joy that night.

With a smile on her lips at the memory, Jamie walked towards one of the bars. Tempted as she was by the multi-colored cocktails, she chose a small glass of white wine and took it to stand on the edge of the dance area, scanning the crowd.

Most wore masks, some attached over their faces while others held them on long poles in the Venetian way. Those who wanted to be recognized held their masks casually, but most were incognito.

A couple spun past on the dance floor, the woman in an ice-white dress, her face masked in branches of icicles, her lips painted blue. Her partner was a Green Man, his face obscured by the leaves of the pagan god. There were men in the crowd with the long nose masks of the Scaramuccia, a rogue and adventurer from the Venetian Commedia Dell'Arte. The wearers had a swagger that matched their characters. Two women walked past in steampunk half-masks of copper and rivets, cogs and wheels, extravagant Victorian dress with bustles and petticoats. The flash of photographers captured everything, some attendees striking coquettish poses and others turning away from the light.

The masquerade ball was the society event of the season and Jamie was aware of how her outfit was nothing compared to some in the room. She wore a black chiffon dress with layers that flowed around her legs, with a bodice in a peacock feather design. A matching butterfly mask hid the upper part of her face with its gauzy wings. It fitted well and although extravagant on her budget, Jamie looked forward to wearing the outfit at tango another night. The feeling of the dress swishing around her legs as she walked made her want to dance, but tonight she was here to watch.

A man walked past in white tie, his black suit tailored to perfection, the lining bright scarlet. He turned and Jamie saw that he wore the mask of the Devil, his face half perfect angel, the other half a demon with twisted features.

She knew the one she sought wouldn't wear such a mask. His peculiar fetish for flesh made him a demon in her mind, but he would no doubt be as mundane as other criminals she had encountered in her years in the police. Yet she wanted the man to come tonight, and she wanted to face him in the darkness.

Jamie found it easy enough to spot the police and security guards in the crowd, their bodies alert, eyes scanning the people before them. Some had no masks, their earpieces marking them out in an obvious fashion, but there were others who wore plain black masks and tuxedos in an attempt to blend in.

A couple spun past as the music sped up. The man wore an eagle mask, its body between his eyes and up onto his forehead, its wings stretching up to meet above his head like a prayer. A woman wore a ragged blue dress, ripped off one shoulder and stained with blood. Her mask looked as if it had been carved from her skin, wet and dripping. In any other setting, Jamie would be rushing to her aid, but the woman's dark smile as she turned heads made it clear she was dressed to win one of the costume prizes for the night.

Jamie understood this craving to be both seen and disguised. It was how she felt at tango, a separate being from her daytime self when she could let the wild side out and not be restrained by society. Masks are used to de-individuate, so the person behind is lost and they can behave as they might want to in a world with no consequences. There were masks that revealed and there were masks that concealed, and as the night darkened and wine flowed, it became evident why some chose concealment. As the alcohol loosened inhibitions, the dark corners became havens for couples locked together in momentary escape.

Jamie had arranged to meet Blake under the trapeze artist, so she made her way through the crowd. It parted for a moment and she saw him, looking up at the performers.

His suit was understated, a perfect tailored fit showing off broad shoulders and wide chest. His mask was black leather and it looked soft enough to touch. He turned, sensing her presence. His stunning blue eyes met hers, framed by the leather mask, and Jamie couldn't help but go to him.

"You look lovely," Blake said softly, bending to her ear so she could hear above the band. Jamie beamed, twirling her skirts a little.

"Glad you like it," she said. "You don't look bad yourself."

"Shame it's not actually a date then." Blake smiled and Jamie blushed a little, staring out into the crowd, avoiding his gaze. "How do you want to manage tonight?" he asked, changing the subject.

"There are plenty of security guards here for any obvious trouble," Jamie said. "But I want us to focus more on potential victims. I'm sure the man will be here tonight. How could he stay away?"

Two women walked past, their low-backed dresses framing their tattoos – one a stylized tree growing out from her spine, and the other of bright fish splashing in a pool of blue.

"Any skin fetishist is going to get off tonight, that's for sure," Blake said. "So we just walk around and keep an eye out?"

"I guess so," Jamie said. "I don't even know what we're looking for." Her voice trailed off as she gazed into the throng, the myriad colors and textures creating ever-shifting patterns in the great hall, a moving work of art.

They walked together around the edges of the crowd as the band wound up its final song of the set. The bass made Jamie's heart thump in time and she could see that Blake longed to get out there and dance. Part of her wanted to forget the case and let loose together, darkness and music and collective energy freeing them from daylight responsibilities. Neither of them had any reason to hold back from each other, did they?

Applause erupted as the band finished up and the lead singer left the stage. Then the lights dimmed and a young black woman walked out, her silver dress sparkling as she moved. She took hold of the microphone and began to sing, her voice rich and powerful as she told of rivers running deep and forsaken love. Couples merged together as her accompaniment joined in, the song lifting the emotion of the crowd.

Blake turned and leaned down, his breath against Jamie's ear. She shivered at the sensation.

"Will you dance with me?" he whispered, his gloved hand taking hers, moving so close that all she had to do was take one tiny step and she would be pressed against him. Jamie's heart thumped in her chest. He smelled of pine needles and spice and all she wanted was to be in his arms.

A moment's hesitation and then she took that tiny step.

She wrapped her arms around his strong back, her cheek against his chest as he held her. One of his gloved hands cradled the back of her head against him, the other stroked her lower back slightly above her buttocks. The song intensified and they swayed together. Jamie pressed her full length against him and she heard him catch his breath.

She looked up and met his eyes. They were dark and intense, filled with a stark need that matched her own. Jamie tilted her head slightly, lifting her mouth to his as he leaned down to kiss her.

CHAPTER 19

A FLICKER IN HER peripheral vision made Jamie stop and pull away.

Through a crack in the crowd she saw a man in an ivory plague doctor's mask on the opposite side of the room. The long beak had been filled with herbs when the sixteenth-century doctors had treated the plagues, but the nightmar-ish figures reeked of death. The man wore a long black cloak that billowed behind as he stalked through the crowd. Jamie thought she recognized something of his walk, but she couldn't quite grasp who she was reminded of.

The moment was broken and Blake turned to see what she was looking at. Jamie felt the loss of his touch but plea-sure would have to wait.

"There," she said, nudging Blake to look across the room, but the man had slipped away in the crowd.

"I don't see anything," Blake said. "What was it?"

"A man in a plague doctor's mask," Jamie said.

Blake's jaw tightened as he scanned the crowd.

"Let's go in opposite directions around the perimeter," Jamie said. "See if we can spot him again."

Blake looked down at her, his face in shadow but his concern evident. He stroked her cheek with one gloved finger. "Don't challenge him, Jamie. Please. Get one of the security guards if you find him first."

"Don't worry," she said. "We don't even know if it's him. It is a masked ball, after all, and the plague doctor is a commonly used mask."

"I'll meet you back here then," Blake said, turning and slipping back into the crowd, his posture resolute.

Jamie began to walk slowly in the opposite direction, scanning the crowd.

***

The mask was heavy but the freedom of anonymity was worth the pain. Dale Cameron stalked around the perimeter of the ball, his eyes flicking over the skin of those dancing close by. There was plenty to tempt him tonight.

In the whirl of the dance, he saw the glazed eyes and wide smiles of intoxication. In the corners of the hall, couples were already indulging in the pleasures of the flesh and on their skin, the marks of the tattooist's trade. But he couldn't stop to admire the body art of the deviants right now. He had other plans for this masquerade. He looked at his watch. It was almost time.

He had been down earlier to inspect the security procedures as part of his day-job role and had brought the bag in then. No one would think to question a Detective Superintendent, after all. Now it was under his cloak and all he had to do was position it, then leave.

***

The band reached a crescendo and the excited crowd screamed and whistled their appreciation. Then the lead singer pointed up to the roof above. The main lights went out and spotlights lit up a net of black and white balloons above.

"Ten ... nine," the crowd shouted.

The countdown to midnight had begun, when the balloons would be released. Inside were all kinds of prizes, tickets to other events, luxury gifts and getaways. Jamie anticipated craziness on the central dance floor as people dove for the balloons, and she moved as far to the edge of the crowd as possible. There, she stood next to one of the huge pillars that supported the main hall.

"Eight ... seven."

Her leg brushed against something and Jamie looked down to see a black package resting against the pillar. Cold sweat prickled across her skin. She looked around quickly for a security guard. Something was very wrong here.

"Six ... five."

She shouted a warning to move, but the attention of the crowd was on the balloons above and the band played so loudly, it was impossible to hear anything. She couldn't see any of the security team near her, but there would be a team by the door. Jamie slid around the back of the crowd, making for the exit as fast as she could.

"Four ... three."

In the flash of the spotlights sweeping the room, Jamie spotted the man in the plague doctor mask walking towards the main exit in front of her. One of his hands reached into the pocket of his cloak.

Jamie pushed her way through the crowd after him, her heart hammering in her chest.

"Two ... one."

On the final count, the crowd screamed in excitement and drums beat faster as the balloons dropped and the scramble for prizes began. The spotlights swept around the room faster now, whirling in crazy patterns with strobes that took the atmosphere to an edge of hysteria.

The man turned, surveying the room, his demeanor that of a judge pronouncing a death sentence.

Jamie emerged at the edge of the crowd. He saw her and met her eyes as she took another step towards him. Jamie felt a spark of recognition as the man turned away and walked swiftly out the exit, as a blast shook the building and the screams of the excited crowd turned to terror.

CHAPTER 20

Screams echoed across the darkness of the Turbine Hall as another blast boomed, followed by the crash of falling masonry.

The explosions were concentrated at the back of the hall right by the stage, where the crowd was the most dense. Jamie was torn – she desperately wanted to pursue the man in the mask, but Blake was back there in the darkness along with hundreds of other people. This was her community now.

She turned back into the hall.

The shouts of the security team could be heard above the din of suffering and those who could walk began to stream for the exits. The dull green emergency lighting cast sickly shadows on their skin, the masks turning them into escapees from a demonic realm. Sirens wailed outside as police and ambulances arrived, the central location at least guaranteeing a swift emergency response.

Jamie joined the security team, helping people to the exits as she searched in growing desperation for Blake at the back of the hall.

Body parts lay strewn on the floor amongst pieces of rubber from the balloons, some limbs perfectly intact but ripped from their owners. The bombs had contained tiny ball bearings which acted as bullets in the blast. Jamie brushed back tears as she stepped around the edge of the horror.

She had to find Blake.

In triage mode, Jamie stepped through the bodies. Some people were groaning, clutching bloody limbs, others were silent, staring straight ahead. She reached down to check one woman's pulse, her face painted white with dust, her eyes open but unblinking. This one was dead. The couple Jamie had seen dancing earlier lay entwined together a little further in. The top half of their bodies were intact, his eagle mask still perfectly placed and nestling into her neck. But their torsos had separated from their legs and they lay in a pool of blood.

Jamie pushed aside her desire to run from the horror, calling on her police training to face what lay head. She focused on her search for Blake, checking bodies, rapidly becoming inured to the dead and dying. Around her the paramedics worked quickly and bodies were stretchered away. London was ever ready for disaster, but it had been years since it had visited the capital in such terrible carnage. Jamie's resolve hardened every second, for every body she checked, for every life that was taken. She would find the man in the mask.

At the very back of the hall, Jamie found a huddle of people behind the stage. The metal structure had shielded them from the airborne missiles and they weren't seriously injured. Blake lay amongst them, blood trickling from the side of his mask to the floor, his blue eyes dazed. Jamie rushed to him, gathering him into her arms, tears coming at last as she lay in the dust at his side.

"Oh, Blake," she whispered. "I thought …"

He pulled her into his arms and she heard his heartbeat against her cheek.

"It's OK," he whispered. "I'm not going anywhere."

***

She had been in too many hospitals lately, Jamie thought a few hours later. She sat in another waiting room drinking crappy coffee, watching the minutes tick by until Blake could be discharged. He only had a concussion but she was well aware of how much more serious it could have been.

A TV in the corner played the early-morning news on a ten-minute repeat cycle, images from the aftermath of the explosion cut together with smartphone footage shot earlier in the evening and uploaded by eager partiers. The parade of beautiful faces in glorious gowns, smiles under their masks, made the after images of body bags and billowing smoke even more shocking. The media was already calling it the Bloody Masquerade.

The news came on again and this time, the images were live. Dale Cameron's patrician face was somber as he read from a prepared statement by the police.

"This morning we mourn the sixty-four people lost last night in the tragedy at the Tate Modern. Over one hundred remain in hospital, some critically injured. My team is processing the crime scene and we're confident that we will be able to bring the terrorists responsible to justice in the following days." He looked directly into the cameras. "We *will* clean up the city, and that's a promise I personally intend to keep."

The camera flicked back to the newsreader.

"That was Detective Superintendent Dale Cameron, who is heading up the task force for the masquerade attack. He's also running for London Mayor in the elections early next week. His main rival, Amanda Masters, was critically injured at the masquerade ball which she was attending as patron of the arts in Southwark."

Jamie's eyes narrowed as she looked at the screen, focusing on Cameron's stance. There was something there, a camouflage of respectability, a hard edge that people wanted but that she knew hid a dangerous side. That kind of strength attracted people and made him a pillar of society, but how far did he take his crusade to clean up the city? Jamie thought back to the night in the Hellfire Caves when she had thought she had seen him in the smoke, part of those who dismembered a man in the darkness. And he had definitely been connected to RAIN, a group who used the mentally ill for their own research ends, uncaring of the human cost. Could Cameron be the man in the mask?

The waiting room door opened and Blake came back in, a dressing on the side of his head. There were dark shadows under his eyes and she saw exhaustion there that reflected her own. She went to him and took his hand.

"I'm taking you home," she said. "By taxi, not by bike."

He smiled. "Thought you said it wasn't a date."

Jamie gave a sharp laugh. "Guess that concussion isn't too bad then."

***

After a short taxi ride, Jamie pushed open the door to Blake's flat in the historic Bloomsbury area. The early-morning commuters were walking through the streets, but it was still quiet in the square. Many of the tall terraced houses were affixed with blue plaques commemorating the famous names who once lived here: Darwin, Dickens and even JM Barrie, who created Peter Pan. As Jamie helped Blake inside and up the staircase, she considered that he was a kind of Lost Boy, his beautiful face wracked by pain from past lives that were not even his own. He mounted the stairs slowly, gripping the bannister with his gloved hand.

Blake's rooms were at the very top of the building, a small studio flat nestled in the eaves with a view over the rooftops of London. It was sparsely furnished with a few pieces of wooden furniture. Jamie had been here once before, when she had been crazy with grief and Blake had been out of his mind on tequila. He had looked after her then, and she would help him now.

"Shall I make tea?" Jamie asked, as Blake sat heavily on the bed.

"You don't have to stay, you know," he said. "I'm only going to sleep."

Jamie smiled. "You have concussion, you idiot. I'm staying while you sleep so you don't suddenly die. After all that trouble finding you after the explosion, do you think I'm going to let you out of my sight now?"

Blake managed to return a smile that turned into a grimace as pain crossed his face. He lay back on the bed and closed his eyes, exhaling slowly.

Jamie crossed to the little kitchen, searching in the cupboards for teabags. She found a mostly empty bottle of tequila next to the Tetley. As she made the tea, she noticed another empty bottle of spirits in the recycling. She knew Blake drank, but she hadn't really realized how much until now. He was damaged, but then so was she. They just coped with their grief in different ways.

She carried the sweet milky tea back to Blake, putting it on a side table within his reach. Jamie sat down on the edge of the bed for a moment, looking down at him. The soft morning light from the window touched his face, his caramel skin smooth and unblemished, his stubble almost a beard now. His chest rose and fell rhythmically but every breath was controlled, forced through the pain of bruising to his chest.

If he had been in a different place when the blast went off … Jamie couldn't think of losing Blake that way. After all, he'd only been there because she'd asked him to be and she had put him in danger before. Images of broken bodies came to her mind, the Turbine Hall full of smoke and the bloody corpses of those who had been celebrating only moments before. The full force of the tragedy began to settle upon her now. It seemed surreal, the sensation similar to how she had felt after Polly's death. The realization of obliteration, how fragile we really are on the face of the earth, how easily ended.

Blake opened his eyes and the deep blue was intense as he gazed up at Jamie. He raised one gloved hand to her cheek, touching her face softly.

"Will you lie down next to me?" His voice was soft with a note of vulnerability. "You must be exhausted too."

At his words, Jamie felt a wave of tiredness wash over her. The last few days had been crazy and the events of last night had almost broken her. This was not how she had imagined them being together, but right now, they both needed a human touch.

"As long as you don't think this is a date," Jamie whispered with a half smile, but she felt the prick of tears in her eyes. She lay down next to him, putting her head on the crook of his shoulder, her hand on his broad chest. Blake smelled of smoke and antiseptic and underneath, his own musky scent. Jamie nuzzled closer, he put his arm around her and they slept.

CHAPTER 21

DALE CAMERON BREATHED A sigh of relief as he walked through his front door and shut it firmly behind him. He was alone at last after the hours of media frenzy that followed the explosion at the Tate. He was still very much awake though – the exhilaration of running rings around the whole lot of them made sure of that.

He stood on the brown welcome mat and took off his brogues, adding them to the shoe rack against the left wall, making sure that they were aligned correctly. He put on his inside shoes, a soft pair of leather moccasins that molded to his feet and allowed him to walk silently on the wooden floors further inside. He hung up his overcoat, adjusting the sleeves so they draped nicely on the peg. He put his keys in the red bowl on the dresser, enjoying the jingling sound as they fell.

Entering his domain was a ritual he relished, especially after a day in the grime of London. When he had cleaned up the city to the point where it was as perfect as his house, his job would be done. And he had made a good start to that in the last twenty-four hours.

He paused by the two portraits that hung side by side in his hallway. His mother's beauty had been captured in a candid shot when he was a child, his own smiling face next to hers as she hugged him close. He had been eleven when she had died of internal injuries sustained after falling down the stairs. He knew what she had been running from, but the police looked after their own and back then, fewer questions were asked about injuries in the home. Dale lifted a finger to her face, as he did every time he came home.

Next to it was a picture of his father, taken in uniform at the height of his career, his face confident. "I have already surpassed you," Dale whispered. Once he was Mayor he would go to that stinking old people's home and spit the words in his father's dying face. That day would come soon now.

Dale smiled at the thought and padded into his study at the back of the house. It was the very model of what a Detective's room should look like, with leather wing chairs, a large oak table and bookshelves with all the latest forensic tomes as well as older first editions behind glass panels. A cigar box sat on the desk and Dale adjusted it so the edges lined up perfectly with the tabletop edge.

He walked to the drinks cabinet and poured himself a generous measure of 62 Gun Salute, one of the best of the Royal Salute whiskeys. Tonight he deserved to celebrate. The list of the dead included noted homosexuals, social justice campaigners, tattoo artists and liberals of every kind. If only that bitch Amanda Masters had died in the blast, but then, perhaps that would have made her some kind of martyr.

He padded behind the desk to one of the bookshelves. He pulled out an Arthur Conan Doyle volume and typed a code onto a hidden keypad. There was an audible click and Dale tugged on the bookcase, revealing a door behind. He pulled a key from around his neck, one he kept hidden under his clothes and on his person at all times. His heart beat faster as he inserted the key in the lock and twisted it slowly, prolonging the pleasure of the moment.

Keeping this place was risky, but a man had to have a

way to commemorate his successes and relive his pleasures. Dale needed a sanctuary away from the world, when he could be his real self. It was a tremendous effort balancing the demands of the police with his real agenda. There were those he worked with on other plans, but the group had been damaged in the wake of the Hellfire Caves scandal and the investigation into RAIN had further weakened the inner circle. But now he was close to power and soon they would rally again.

He pushed open the door and entered the small room, flicking a switch to turn on the lights that illuminated certain parts of his collection. One wall was dedicated to masks and Dale reached out to touch the plague doctor's hooked beak. He had replaced it after his success at the masquerade ball. The city was infected with a plague and it was time to weed out the weak and the needy, those who were a burden on society. Nature knew how to cull the herd, he only helped the process with his bombs.

Next to the mask were his knives, some ceremonial and precious for their monetary value. But others … Dale walked to the display and caressed the gleaming edge of the skinning knife. This one held greater pleasure than much of his collection, but now he would have to rest it for a while. He would soon give up control of crime scenes as Mayor and no longer have the ability to disappear evidence. The knife would have to remain on the wall, at least for now.

He ran his fingers over the books of human skin that were placed on their own bookshelf, flesh against flesh as their covers touched. Each was a slightly different size, all the better to allow the tattoos to be fully displayed on the covers and spine. There was space missing for the book he would have had made from the skin that had been found at the old abattoir. It was in the evidence room now, but perhaps there would be a way to get it back once the noise had died down.

Owning a Cabinet of Obscene Objects had once been fashionable amongst aristocratic families. So many of the treasures of antiquity portrayed sex and debauchery that special rooms were created to protect the eyes of the more sensitive members of society. Dale thought of this place as his own cabinet, where only the strong could stomach what was within. Not that he ever allowed anyone inside. The bachelor life suited him just fine.

He turned and bent to his prize possession, his pulse racing as he placed his hands upon the box. It was carved with images of carnal depravity, one of those objects that the public would complain of while secretly craving a look. As part of the police task force on pornography, he had overseen the seizure of millions of photos and videos over the years. He had kept a selection of it to add to his own collection, not for his own pleasure of course, but to galvanize his desire to stamp out the perverts who made them. Only by understanding their mindset could he seek them out and destroy them.

He had also kept copies of crime scene photos, finding a beauty in the colors and poses of corpses. He opened the box, his hand hovering over his pictures. He wanted to allow himself the time to sit and gaze at them, to find his own pleasure in the descent into depravity. But he had more work to do today. He pulled out four new photos from his jacket pocket. Each one was a close-up of a corpse from the Turbine Hall, three women and a man, each body ripped apart but their faces intact. Dale liked beauty with an edge of darkness and these epitomized his particular fascination.

He sat down on the single chair in the room, an antique he had purchased from the estate of Sir Francis Galton, the esteemed eugenicist, a man who had known about culling the weak. Dale liked to think he could channel the great man here somehow. He breathed deeply and took another sip of his whiskey. Now that he had the mandate of the city to pursue those responsible for the Masquerade Massacre, it was time to send a stronger signal. He had been preparing for this day for a long time and finally he could act with public support behind him. In the next week, he would rid London of its dregs and take the Mayoralty on a surge of public support for strong-armed action.

He thought back to the Turbine Hall in the moments before the explosion. He had turned to fix the masquerade in his mind, seeing the hall through the slits in his mask, framed as a tableau of revelry. The proud before the fall. But someone had seen him. There was no way Jamie Brooke could have recognized him in the mask, but he had felt a moment of connection between them.

She had been a thorn in his side for too long now. Her interference had brought down the Lyceum that night in the Hellfire Caves and she had stumbled into the plans RAIN had for the mentally ill. Dale remembered their confrontation after that case. He had wanted her reassigned somewhere she would be kept busy and out of the way, but she had resigned and started her own investigation service. She couldn't be allowed to threaten his plans, but there were ways she could be dealt with this time and it might help rid him of the others too.

Dale pulled out his wallet and riffled through it, finding the business card with a blue boxing glove on it. He picked up the phone and dialed. He would start with Southwark, his own rotten borough. If he picked off the leaders, the rest would fall.

CHAPTER 22

THE SMASHING OF GLASS woke Magda from a deep sleep. Her heart beat fast at the unusual sound, panic rising in her chest. She untangled herself from O's sleeping form and pulled a robe around herself. She walked quickly into the studio area to find flames spreading from a broken bottle of accelerant, glass all over the floor from the broken window.

The fire caught on some of the flammable paint and flames spread quickly towards the stack of canvases in the corner.

"Olivia," Magda shouted. "Get up, quickly. We have to get out." She grabbed at some of the canvases nearest to her, dragging them out of the way of the flames, but she knew it was too late. The fire was spreading too fast.

The high-pitched squeal of the smoke alarm pierced the air, a note of danger and desperation. Magda beat at the flames with a fire blanket, sobbing as she watched her canvases catch and burn.

O emerged from the bedroom and rushed into the kitchenette to grab the fire extinguisher. But Magda knew that it was only meant for a small fire and sure enough, it was soon empty, the flames still spreading. She called the emergency services, giving the address in a calm voice and explaining the situation, even as her mind struggled to fathom the destruction around her. The soothing voice of the operator assured her that the fire brigade was on its way, but Magda knew it would be too late.

"We have to get out." O tugged at her lover's arm, covering her mouth to block some of the smoke.

"I can't leave it all," Magda whispered in desperation. "This is everything. I'll be ruined."

O put her hand on Magda's cheek, turning her face and looking into her eyes.

"*You* are everything, my love. This stuff can be replaced, but you can't. Haven't we learned that over the last days?"

Magda looked around at the flaming studio, her canvases, her equipment on the way to ruin. This was her life's work, her sanctuary. The flames roared as they accelerated through a pile of packaging material.

"We have to get out now." O pulled on her arm and Magda's resolve crumbled. With tears in her eyes, she stumbled out of the studio and into the courtyard outside. Groups of people stood looking on, tenants from the flats above weeping as the flames climbed higher and they were pushed back towards the road beyond.

The sound of cracking and buckling beams could be heard from within as an upper level collapsed down through the ceilings to the ground floor. The creaking protests of the building were like the groans of the dying.

Magda stood as close she could, the heat from the fire almost burning her skin. In other circumstances she would have reveled in these flames, an element of destruction that allowed rebirth. She had thrown her own past on flames like these, destroying what was spent and rotten to enable the new to arise. But now … everything she had built here would be destroyed. She swallowed, fighting to hold back the tears.

The sound of sirens filled the air and fire engines arrived

along with police to control the scene. Tenants and onlookers were pushed further back, urged to move away but Magda couldn't leave. She watched as fire hoses began to soak the flames, their powerful jets raining down on her studio. Whatever hadn't been lost in the fire would be destroyed by its opposite element. Perhaps there was a lesson in that.

O slipped an arm round Magda's waist, leaning her head on her lover's shoulder.

"There's nothing we can do here," she said. "Why don't you come back to my place? Have a drink. We'll come back when it's all under control."

But Magda couldn't tear her eyes from the flames.

"I need to stay," she said, her voice quiet. She turned and looked into O's eyes. She was so lucky to have this woman in her life, but there were times when she needed to be alone. "But maybe you can go get some supplies. Hot chocolate would be good. Maybe something stronger to go with it."

O leaned up and kissed her full on the mouth.

"Of course, I won't be long."

O turned and navigated through the crowd away from the scene. Magda walked to the edge of the perimeter and sat down on a step, exhaling deeply as she looked into the flames again, holding out her hands to the fire so she could see the full length of her own tattoos, silhouetted against the orange-red of the flames. The marks on her skin were both the end and the beginning, she thought, remembering the past. Had it all been worth it?

She had left Ireland twenty-two years ago now – strange that it had been so long. It seemed like a different life.

Back then, her name had been Ciara, for her dark hair and for the saint who saved a village from fire back in the seventh century. Raised in a strict Catholic home and sent to a convent school, her world had been shuttered and controlled by rules. Any question deemed wrong for a girl to ask had resulted in punishment, and she had spent a lot of time recovering from the birch in the struggle to be silent.

Boys were forbidden and exciting, although she had sensed more of an attraction to girls even back then. The nights she had escaped the convent and spent drinking with the local boys had turned into something more, and when she discovered she was pregnant, her world turned. She was called deviant and possessed by the Devil for following the path of sin. Magda remembered how confused she had been back then, how angry that fumbling and pain had resulted in something that turned her into a pariah. Even now, she could still recall the hate in the Reverend Mother's eyes as she had been cast out.

They had sent her to a house for unwed mothers to await the arrival of the child, but Magda knew she couldn't stay. She had felt an overwhelming sense that she would die there if she remained. The eyes of the other girls were hollow and haunted, rumors of a pit out the back where hundreds of babies and young mothers were buried, taken back to God.

That night she had run from the place, escaping over the fields and heading cross country, eventually reaching the coast. There she had used her body to bargain for a ferry crossing, the pregnancy not yet far gone enough to put the man off. She didn't care for the sexual act, but she certainly understood what it was worth.

Once on English soil, she had found an abortion clinic. When they asked for her name, she found herself saying Magda. The harsh syllables were more European than Irish and yet Mary Magdalene had always been the saint she had loved the most. The sinner who Jesus had loved, the woman whom he chose to reveal himself to first in the garden after his resurrection.

Magda looked down at her tattoos. The ink reclaimed her body, but it had taken many years to get to the point where she accepted all of herself. Sex was the only trade she had when she arrived in London, and she had become the very sinner that the nuns claimed she was. But the sex was mechanical, and never meant anything except cash to live on. It was work, and easy enough. There had been some bastards but most were lonely men who needed to be touched, and she had understood their need for love and acceptance.

Perhaps she had always loved women, but she hadn't even known it was allowed until London, the city that welcomed all. She had found her tribe here, the sex workers, the junkies, the pagans, those who society had labeled deviant but really just didn't conform. A cast of antiheroes against the backdrop of the greatest city on earth.

The Magdalene had been her first tattoo, embodying both sinner and saint in her many incarnations. She was also separate from the Mother figure, the Mary who Magda could only pity. The Mother had no identity apart from her relationship to the Son and Magda couldn't ever see herself living like that. But the Magdalene – now there was a woman worth admiring.

The flames were dying down now, finally under control by the fire service. Above her, Magda heard the cawing of the ravens. The birds wheeled high in the sky but Magda could still feel her connection to them. Sometimes it was as if she saw with their eyes. Her other full-sleeve tattoo was for them, her totem birds, and for the Morrigan, the Celtic goddess of battle who roamed on the wings of ravens, choosing those who would die and those who would live again.

On the day the tattoos had been finished, Magda finally felt her own transformation had completed. She tied herself to her Irish-Catholic roots in one way, but her own truth was bound up in the strong female goddess. On that day, she had walked away from sex work – but not from sex workers. This borough was her home now, and her work as an urban shaman was to bring that sense of the otherworld to the physical. But was she too attached to what she had created here, and was this a way to leave it all behind again? Was it time to turn her back on London and seek peace somewhere new?

There was a deep booming sound as thunder rolled across the night sky and it began to rain. Magda turned her face to the sky, letting the drops wash her tears away as she sent up a prayer to the goddess of the dark, she of the moon, the Maiden and the Crone.

"Help me," Magda whispered.

Ash ran in rivulets around her feet now, remnants of her art mingling with the structure of the building. It would soon flow into the Thames, the droplets becoming one with the great river that kept the city alive. Magda smiled. Her own ashes would be scattered there one day. It was a reminder that all would perish but this city would stand, whatever came.

As the rain began to hammer down, Magda huddled back into the doorway. Some of the crowd dispersed while others put up colored umbrellas, their faces in shadow. O returned, juggling an umbrella and a bulging paper bag. She crouched on the step next to Magda, sheltering them both from the downpour.

"Here," O said, pulling out two steaming cups of hot chocolate. "Sugar makes everything better." She dug back in the bag and pulled out a large chocolate brownie. "Overdosing on it must seriously help." Magda gave a half smile as they broke the cake in two and shared the pieces, watching as the firefighters finished dowsing the flames and the rain dampened any last embers. The sweet taste in her mouth made Magda focus on that moment, how grateful she was to be alive, to have O by her side.

"Thank you," she said, turning to kiss O's cheek. Her words contained a promise for a future, whatever that would look like.

"We'll take it a day at a time," O said. "You'll create new

work soon enough, and you can stay with me until we find you a new studio. The insurance will cover it, although I know the money won't replace your art." She paused, gazing into the ruins that lay before them. "What do you think they'll do with this site? Rebuild the studios?"

Magda stiffened as realization dawned. "This block is owned by the same corporation that has been trying to turn the social housing into luxury flats. They've been trying to get us out for years. Now there'll be no more annoying tenants to deal with."

"You don't think –" O's words trailed off, her blue eyes clouding. "Oh no – what if this isn't the only place under attack?" She dug through her bag. "I haven't been checking my phone." She pulled it out. There were ten missed calls and texts.

O stood up, her face pale. "I need to get to the Kitchen."

CHAPTER 23

THEY CAME BEFORE DAWN, black balaclavas over their heads to hide their faces from the ever-present CCTV cameras and matching black clothing with no identifying marks. One of them carried a baseball bat, another one hefted a tire iron, banging it against his palm. The other two held no obvious weapons, but their meaty hands were clenched into fists. They all wore thick-soled work boots. "The uniform of the militia," their leader called it. They were working together to clean up the city and as long as the police powers were curtailed by bureaucracy, this was the only way the deviants could be dealt with.

They were silent as they approached the Kitchen, their steps deliberate, single-minded. One of them jimmied the lock, breaking open the door and allowing them into the space. The smell of roasting meat hung in the air, a homely smell that made one of the men briefly reconsider what they had come to do. The leader took charge, gesturing as he spoke.

"You and you – get to work on the cooking facilities. I want everything destroyed so it can't be easily fixed. No fire here though, only damage. You – with me out the back."

Two of the men got to work in the kitchen. One unplugged the chest freezer, opening the lid to reveal containers of stew, cuts of meat and bags of vegetables. He grabbed a huge bottle of bleach from the cleaning supplies and poured it over the food. *No dinner for the dole bludgers*, he thought. Then he turned to the double fridge, swinging the baseball bat as he walked. *Time to break some shit.* The man smiled with pleasure.

Another man began to systematically destroy the inner workings of all the equipment in the large kitchen. With his electrical and engineering background, he understood it wasn't about brute force and smashing things. It was about twisting wires and cutting supply lines and melting specific elements that were hard and expensive to replace. It would take them weeks to get this place running again.

In the storeroom, the leader opened the back doors to reveal the small truck they'd arrived in.

"Everything needs to go," he said, pointing at the shelves full of canned and packaged food, boxes of fruit and vegetables. "Empty the place and we'll dump it all on the way home."

They began shifting the pallets, loading them into the truck as sounds of muted destruction came from the kitchen.

It soon began to rain, the overcast skies breaking. The leader looked up at the clouds. It would be heavy enough to help firefighters calm the flames from the studio they had torched earlier.

"Let's get a move on," he said. "We need to get out of here."

As they finished packing the last of the boxes into the van, a young man rounded the corner, approaching the entrance to the Kitchen. He was blonde, with a blue streak through his hair. He had his hands in his pockets and a half smile on his lips.

The men in the shadowed parking area stood still as he approached. The leader held his hand up, waiting to see whether the young man would pass on, just another local out for a morning walk.

But he stopped at the door of the Kitchen and pulled a set of keys from his pocket. As he reached for the lock, his face fell. He saw the broken lock and reached for his phone.

The leader nodded at two of the men.

They burst from the shadows with no words, only heavy footsteps thumping on the pavement. The young man looked up and saw them, dropping the keys and sprinting away.

The first man was on him in seconds, pushing him to the ground.

"No you don't, you little fag."

He kicked out viciously, slamming his boot into the young man's stomach.

The beating was swift and deliberate, the men knowledgeable on the various subcategories of assault, battery and grievous bodily harm. Within a minute, the young man was unconscious, his beautiful face a bloody mess, his body curled in on itself in pain.

They left him there and ran back to the van, jumping in as it roared off down the road. The rain pooled around the young man's body, washing the blood from his broken skin.

***

O jumped out of the cab and ran towards the door of the Kitchen dodging the puddles. Magda paid the driver and followed her, shielding her face from the heavy rain. As she approached the door, O slipped, dropping her bag. Magda bent to pick it up and as she did so, she saw the body on the pavement further down the street.

Magda dashed to the young man's body, O running after her. Magda felt for the pulse at his neck. It was weak and sputtering. She pulled out her phone and called for an ambulance, giving them the location.

"It's Ed," O said quietly, kneeling by his body, uncaring of the puddles. "He works the morning shift." She bent to his ear. "Hold on," she whispered. "We're here now and help is coming. Hang in there, Ed – please."

Magda reached out a hand and laid it on the young man's chest, willing life into him. Above her, a flock of crows began to gather and circle, their feathers dripping in the rain. Their harsh cawing joined Magda's whispered chant of ancient power as O looked on, her eyes fixed on Ed's pale face.

Within minutes, a yellow and green motorbike swerved around the corner, the distinctive shades of the ambulance service marking it out. In central London, they were mostly on scene faster than the larger vans. The single responder grabbed her bike pack and knelt by Ed's side. As Magda lifted her hand and moved back, the crows settled in a nearby tree, silent now as they watched the scene with narrow black eyes.

"We only recently found him," O said, as the paramedic expertly assessed the wounds, calling on her radio for a full ambulance crew.

"We can't move him," the paramedic said. "And I'm worried about internal bleeding after an assault like this. The police will be here soon to take your statements."

Magda held O's hand as they watched her work. The ambulance arrived and they soon had Ed on a gurney and in the van.

"Where are you taking him?" O asked.

"St Thomas," the paramedic said. "But it will be a while until he comes round."

The police arrived as the ambulance drove off. Two officers emerged from the patrol car, gesturing to O and Magda to stand in the shelter of the nearby houses.

"Didn't we see you earlier?" one of the officers said. "At the fire near Borough Market."

Magda nodded.

"It's been a busy night."

"How about we do the statements inside the Kitchen?" O said. "We can get out of the rain."

They walked back down the street. The door was open a fraction.

"That's unusual," O said. "It should be locked, unless Ed opened it."

One of the officers bent to the lock.

"It's been broken," he said. "We'll go in first."

Magda and O stood back as the officers pushed open the door and proceeded inside. The smell of rancid meat wafted out to them, overlaid with the stink of shit and piss.

O's face contorted with pain and she rushed inside, Magda following.

The police officers stood looking at the wreckage of the place. Every piece of furniture was smashed, every item in the kitchen destroyed, food all over the floor topped with human excrement. The walls were spray painted with graffiti, the black paint dripping globules onto the floor.

Whores. Fags. Deviants. Get out.

The hateful words burned in Magda's mind, somehow worse than the destruction that lay about them.

O fell to her knees, tears streaming down her face. Magda knelt next to her, wrapping her arms around her weeping lover. After a night of staying strong, this final offense had broken them.

CHAPTER 24

IT HAD BEEN A long day.

Blake walked slowly along the crowded streets from the museum back towards his flat. With each step he felt the jarring of the pavement through his bruised body and each breath hurt his lungs. He really should be in bed, but the exhibition opened at the weekend and it was all hands on deck to finish the last pieces of work. He wanted to be part of it.

After the blast at the Tate, Margaret had agreed on time off, but Blake wanted to complete his part of the display, and working alongside Catherine wasn't so difficult. He turned away from the flat and headed for Bar-Barian. Alcohol was the best way he knew to quiet his mind and dull the pain of his injuries.

A couple of drinks to take the edge off.

He walked into the bar, its familiarity a comfort. He didn't have to pretend here, because he was surrounded by people like himself. People who found truth and solace in drink.

"Usual?"

Blake nodded and Seb the barman poured two shots of tequila and grabbed a bottle of Becks from the fridge. Blake downed the shots, letting the golden nectar seep through him, bringing a calm he could reach no other way. He sipped at the beer, checking out the after-work crowd who gathered in Soho to find love for the night, acceptance in the arms of a stranger. Drinking alone in his flat meant that he had a problem, but here he was just one face in a party that went on at all hours in this part of London.

After another couple of shots, Blake sensed the heaviness that would let him slip into dreamless sleep. He wandered home slowly, the few blocks taking longer than usual as he lingered, watching the faces of the passersby. This was the floating part of being happily drunk, a wellbeing that buoyed the spirit.

Maybe he should call Jamie, Blake thought. Maybe she would come over and they would be together. Or he could call Catherine for something altogether less complicated.

He shook his head as he pushed the key into the lock on the front door. Probably best to go to sleep. He walked up the stairs, his steps heavy.

Then stopped at the top of the stairs. Something was wrong.

The door to his flat was open a few inches. Someone was here. The drunken sensations subsided as Blake focused. He clutched his keys in his hand, pushing one through his fingers to use as a weapon if needed.

He pushed open the door.

The man from the museum sat on his bed holding the Galdrabók in his strong hands. It was open to a page of Icelandic spells, the man's lips moving as he read them quietly.

He looked up at Blake, his eyes the color of northern oceans that would freeze a man to death in seconds. The scar across his nose was deep, the flesh livid around the edges. He was a stranger, but once again Blake saw a hint of his father in those features.

Blake stood in the doorway, ready to run.

"What are you doing here?" he asked. "Who are you?"

"I've been wanting to read this book again for a long time," the man said, with a slight Scandinavian accent. "Your father stole it from us many years ago."

Blake knew he should give it to the man and let him leave, but he felt a strange possessiveness for it, a need to keep it under his bed like a talisman. His father had used the book and Blake was curious as to whether he could use it himself.

"You don't look much like him." The man smiled, baring teeth that had been filed in the way of the Vikings. "But then I heard Magnus married as far from the north as he could."

"Who are you?" Blake asked again.

"Your uncle," the man said. "Allfrid Olofsson. One of your northern kin."

He held out a hand to Blake, holding it there, waiting. His other hand rested on the Galdrabók, claiming it.

After a moment, Blake reached out with gloved hands and shook. Allfrid looked down at the gloves.

"You have the sight, then."

His words were matter of fact and Blake reeled at the implication. It was the first time that anyone had been so accepting of his gift, treating it as mundane.

"What do you know of it?" he asked, coming into the room now and shutting the door. Allfrid was a threat, of that he was sure, but he also wanted to know more.

"You come from an ancient line of seers," Allfrid said. "But your father wanted none of it. He was scared of the visions and what was demanded of those who could renew the pact with the gods."

Blake sat down heavily in his desk chair.

"My father had visions too?"

Betrayal washed over him. The years of beating, the curses, the claim that Satan had entered him. All were just a way for his father to deny his own gift.

"He was one of the strongest among us," Allfrid said. "At least when we were young. But he left before he understood the true meaning or how to control it."

Blake looked at Allfrid, the words sparking something within.

"Yes, boy." Allfrid understood the look. "You *can* control it. You don't need those gloves if you know how to separate the visions in your mind from reality. You've never been taught the right way."

Blake pulled the gloves from his hands, revealing the crisscross scars underneath.

Allfrid shook his head in resignation. "Your father?"

Blake nodded. "He tried to beat the curse from me. And yet he kept the Galdrabók and used it to draw people to him. Even my mother, I suppose."

"We all have to manage our addictions," Allfrid said. His piercing gaze rocked Blake to the core, as if he could see the alcohol wrapped around his soul. "It's a struggle we each walk alone." He traced a finger over the pages of the book. "But this can help you, as can your family."

He thrust the book towards Blake.

"Read me through it, I know you can do this. Let me show you the north."

Blake hesitated. He had read his father through the book and witnessed a human sacrifice that left him retching and weak. Was he safe in this room, in a city so far from that wilderness?

He sensed a hard edge to Allfrid, a blade's breadth away from savagery, but here in the city it remained cloaked. If he opened his mind to the man, would he be able to return?

But curiosity drove him on. This was the first time anyone had explained his visions as an integral part of him, and now he knew he wasn't alone.

Blake put his hand on the book and closed his eyes.

There was no sinking through the layers of memory this time. There was a pure jolt of energy and he gasped with the cold. Blake opened his eyes to find himself standing in freshly fallen snow surrounded by birch trees. The tinkling of a stream pervaded the glade and a light rain fell on his exposed skin. Above the trees he could see mountaintops.

Blake inhaled deeply. The air was fresh and clean, filling his lungs as a sense of freedom expanded within him. There was nothing of human manufacture in sight, the sounds and smells only spoke of what had been here for millennia.

There was a crunch in the snow behind him and Blake turned to see Allfrid smiling at him.

"This is only the beginning," he said. "But I wanted you to see the place I come to be at peace." He looked up to the mountain. "Your father and I climbed that peak as boys. Back then, he understood the power of the place. But he left and when you're far from nature, you lose touch with its strength."

Blake could hear his own heartbeat in the still of the glade. He could feel the pulse at his neck, his wrists, and he felt a connection to the earth here. He wanted to jump around in the snow, lie back in it and look up at the sky. It was far from the wild, dark places of the New Forest where he had grown up.

Allfrid cupped his hands around his mouth and called into the woods, a harsh sound, the words as raw as the land they stood in.

A few minutes later, faces appeared in the trees and figures crept through the wood, darting between the sheltered spaces. There were children amongst the group as well as older people and those Blake's own age.

One little girl peeked out from a tree close by, catching his eye. She giggled at him and Blake smiled back. He must look odd to them with his dark skin and city clothes. She took a step out into the snow, her hand held out to him in greeting.

As she came closer, Blake reached out to touch the girl's fingers.

A whoosh of cold wind swept snow into his face.

He gasped, opened his eyes, and he was back in the attic flat again. He grabbed the desk with both hands, trying to orient himself into the physical space again.

Allfrid laughed, shaking his head. "You need training, boy, if you're to use your gift properly."

"They could see me," Blake said, his voice shaky. "Those people, they could see me and touch me?"

"Our tribe live with closer ties to outer realms. What you see as a vision, others experience as part of their usual world. You differentiate but that's only because you haven't truly accepted that part of yourself. But every time you read, you take a step towards us. Each time you sink into memory, it also seeps into you. Beware of doing this without the proper training, boy. Come to us and I will show you."

Allfrid rose to his feet, the Galdrabók in his hands. "Now, I must go and I'm taking this." His head almost touched the ceiling in the tiny flat and he bent a little, the posture of a man who was always leaning over others. "The grimoire belongs with the family – but you are one of us."

He pulled a map from his pocket and handed it to Blake. It was marked by lines and runes, with a clear red X in a patch of green in northern Sweden. "The glade is marked. If you come to us, we can teach you of your gift and how to use the book." Allfrid looked out of the window, over the rooftops of London. "Or you can stay here, wearing those gloves to hold back the visions, using alcohol to deaden their power, wondering how you fit into the world." He looked down at Blake again. "It's your choice."

Allfrid turned and walked out of the flat without a backwards glance, leaving Blake sitting on a chair, shaken by the experience of the vision. He heard his uncle's footsteps tramp down the stairs and then the bang of the door onto the street.

CHAPTER 25

JAMIE PUSHED OPEN THE door to her tiny office and picked up the mail from the mat, juggling her coffee cup in the other hand. She wanted this space to keep her work separate from her personal life but once again, the two were mingling. *Perhaps work was life*, she thought. For some people at least. The need to work certainly drove her, and she never wanted to stop. Retirement seemed an outmoded concept from a different time and the day her brain checked out was the day she would stop working. But it was more than the love of the job that kept her going today. After Polly's death, she had lost purpose but there was a glimmer of hope that she might find it again in this community.

The news from Magda this morning had made Jamie determined to dig into the ownership records of the buildings in the Southwark area. Who would stand to gain from the destruction of the studio apartments and who would want the Kitchen closed? Ed was in a stable condition in hospital, but it seemed like the community was being attacked on all fronts.

She opened her laptop and began to search the council databases that held the area's property records. There were layers of holding companies but the trail would be there, Jamie was sure of it. She knew how to investigate into the directors and shareholders of companies from her days in the police and it was only a matter of patience to sift through the levels down to the originators. She sipped her coffee as she searched, copying and pasting lists of names, cross-checking against the Companies database that held the legal records for each UK entity.

After a couple of hours lost in data, Jamie had a broad sense of how many companies were vying for the valuable property in Southwark. Many were registered overseas, but there were names that tied them together. There was a crossover of interest between projects as varied as the Shard construction to Guy's and St Thomas' hospital development and renovation of some of the older warehouses. One name kept coming up: Vera Causa Limited.

Jamie did a quick search and discovered that the Latin words meant True Cause. She began to delve into what she could find about the company, quickly discovering that the shareholding lay in bearer shares. These were physical stock certificates where the owner didn't have to be registered in any way and dividends were disbursed to whoever held the shares. The setup was designed to hide ownership and legislation was currently being debated that would make it illegal. But for now, the owner of these bearer shares could stay hidden. Jamie frowned, taking a last sip of the now-cold coffee.

A sudden commotion and banging from the outer offices broke her concentration.

Jamie emerged from her office to find one of the other tenants shouting at a man in the hallway. The official wore a pinstriped suit, standing with back straight as he taped a notice on the door.

"My contract clearly says that the lease is six months," the tenant exclaimed, waving paperwork at him.

The suit handed a document to the gesticulating man.

"You missed the clause for pest control," he said.

"Everyone needs to be out of here within the next two hours and then fumigation will commence. You won't have access for at least a week, but you'll be contacted when the building is available again."

The tenant continued raging, his protestations useless against immoveable bureaucracy.

Jamie ducked back inside her tiny office, packing up what little paperwork she had started to accumulate into her backpack. There was a nagging doubt in her mind about the timing of the pests and no evidence of them that she could see.

Walking downstairs ten minutes later, she stopped to read the notice from the landlord on the way out. The company name at the bottom was one of those that she had tied back to Vera Causa.

The sun was out as she emerged onto the street. The units were away from the main tourist strip along the Thames, but close enough that she could be amongst people quickly. Jamie appreciated anonymity in the middle of a bustling city. Small communities might protect in some ways, but they also curtailed originality and punished nonconformity. The city allowed all to flourish and anyone could find their niche here, but could it be that Vera Causa was trying to make Southwark compliant in some way? A test case, with the rest of the city to follow.

Walking helped her to think, so Jamie emerged onto the riverside near the Anchor pub and turned west. The grey of the Thames was like quicksilver in the sun, the waters high and lapping against the strong pontoons that held it back from the city. Jamie passed a busker in the Southwark Bridge underpass, the jaunty guitar tune bringing a smile to her face. She dropped a couple of coins into his case, nodding a thankyou. The buskers and street entertainment flourished in the city as the sun came out, the summer months bringing tourists from all over the world. And here in Southwark, busking kept artists from the food banks and brought music to the streets. Doubly wonderful, Jamie thought.

A little further on, she reached the Tate Modern. The old power station with its one tall chimney stood proud on the south bank facing the Millennium Bridge, with the classic dome of St Paul's beyond. But today, the crime scene tape held back curious tourists and the gallery was closed until further notice. Most of the structural damage from the masquerade attack had been at the back of the large Turbine Hall, out of sight from the north view, but Jamie knew what it looked like inside.

Images from that night flashed through her brain, the dead and the dying, her frantic search for Blake.

Her breath came fast and she moved to the edge of the pavement, sitting down on a step for a moment as the dizziness passed. A part of her mind witnessed the panic her body felt. Strange, because she had never experienced this in the police, even as part of the homicide team.

Jamie let the waves of anxiety roll over her as she sat looking out at the ever-shifting waters of the Thames. Perhaps it was precisely because she had no team that she was feeling out of control. She certainly missed having backup and resources. She thought of Missinghall and his enthusiasm, the respect she had earned in the police. Had she been too quick to resign? Could she consider going back?

Feeling calmer now, Jamie walked back to her little apartment complex. If she couldn't work at the office, she'd have to make a space in the flat because the job was really too private to work in a public coffee shop.

Her street was tightly packed with close terraced houses, each one up against the next in a racially mixed community. Jamie spotted a few people standing outside her building. She frowned. That was unusual.

As she approached, she saw the same eviction team that

had been at the office building. But this time there were a couple of enforcer types with the suits, gorilla men with thick biceps and heavy foreheads. The crowd of tenants from the building had been joined by several of the other street residents. Some were angry and others shook their heads in resignation.

"It's temporary," the suited man was saying, his hands held up apologetically. "But you have to be out before midnight. You should be able to get back in within the next week. We'll notify you all."

"What about compensation?"

"You can't do this –"

"My kids need –"

"Where are we meant to go?"

"The faster you get out and we can start the fumigation process, the faster you can all get back in."

Jamie stood on the edge of the crowd. There was no way this was legal, but it would take a lot of energy to fight the powerful corporation that stood behind the eviction notice. It seemed Vera Causa Limited had a long reach, and this definitely felt like it was turning personal. Years in the police had given Jamie a sense when all was not quite as it should be, and she was getting that vibe on overdrive right now. She needed to find out more on Vera Causa, but she couldn't do it here.

She elbowed her way through the crowd.

"I'm in Flat 9," she said to the man on the door.

He grunted and let her through.

Up in her flat, Jamie grabbed a rucksack and filled it with some clothes, grabbing whatever was clean. Looking around, she realized there wasn't much she actually cared about here. Her life wasn't defined by things anymore, but by memories. She picked up the photo of Polly by her bed, her daughter's laughing face captured in a moment without pain. She smiled. She would have done anything to save

Polly, but at least they had experienced happy times together in the short time they had. She wrapped the photo frame in a t-shirt and put it gently in her pack. Vera Causa could take her home and her workplace, but they couldn't take her memories.

Jamie pulled bedsheets out of the cupboard and spread them over the furniture. She was doubtful that they were actually going to fumigate the place but might as well make it look as if she believed the story.

It was getting dark when she emerged outside. The gorilla men stood by the gate and they ticked her name off a list as she confirmed her cellphone number.

"We'll call you as soon as it's all done," one of the men said. "Should be a week at most."

Jamie didn't bother to reply. She headed down the road away from the flat, back towards the center of Southwark.

She had a feeling of being untethered, unsure of what to do next. She could just keep walking. She could get on a train and head to the coast, get on a boat and go to France and on through the continent, or even fly somewhere new. She thought of the freedom she felt dancing tango. South America had always been somewhere she'd wanted to visit. Now she was free to go and the opportunities suddenly seemed endless.

After all, there was no real reason to stay. Was there?

Blake was damaged, and perhaps she had imagined their connection. Establishing her business was an uphill battle and she was only on the edges of the Southwark community right now. They wouldn't even notice she was gone. The thought was freeing but also slightly disconcerting. Jamie knew her independence had kept her from being immersed in a community when she was caring for Polly, and her life was poorer for it now. But the double eviction seemed like a pretty big sign that she wasn't wanted here.

Could she commit to this place when everything seemed to point towards leaving?

Jamie walked down to South Bank and stood looking out at the Thames. The waters ran swiftly towards the ocean, the eddies making patterns in the current. Flotsam and jetsam, pieces of the discarded city, caught on the boats moored in the central channel. They were pinned for a moment, crushed against the metal and then dragged under or whipped around the side by the fast-moving river. Then they drifted on towards the sea.

Jamie exhaled slowly, then pulled out her phone and dialed.

CHAPTER 26

O ANSWERED ON THE second ring.

"Jamie, are you OK?"

Jamie smiled at the caring note in O's voice. She did have friends here, and right now her friends were hurting too.

"Actually, I've been evicted."

"What the hell is going on?" O's frustration echoed Jamie's own. "Why don't you come over here? You can kip on the couch, if that's alright. Magda's here too."

"Thank you," Jamie said. "I'll be there in twenty minutes."

***

O's flat was chaotic. Magda stood in the middle of the living area surrounded by the few canvases that hadn't been destroyed in the fire. She held out one of her crow photographs to Jamie, the edges of one corner burned and curled, the black bubbled up beneath the feathers.

"I think I might have found a new technique," Magda said, her laugh with an edge of mania. She shook her head. "But this is all I have left from ten years in that studio."

O swept out of the kitchen, a large glass of red wine in either hand.

"You have your wonderful mind left, my love." She

handed one glass to Magda and the other to Jamie. "And you both have my flat. What's not to like?"

She turned back into the kitchen, emerging with her own large glass and the rest of the bottle.

Jamie couldn't help but smile at O's optimism. In the face of everything they were going through, it seemed she still saw a positive side.

O looked at her watch.

"Quick, turn on the telly. The announcement about the Mayor should be on any minute."

The familiar sounds of the BBC news jingle filled the flat and they watched in silence as the announcement was made. Even O couldn't summon anything positive to say as they watched Dale Cameron step forward to accept the position.

Jamie felt a stone settle in the pit of her stomach, a heavy sense of dread. Riding high on a right-wing ticket of cleaning up the city, Cameron's patrician face was all smiles and promises, but part of her knew that he was entwined in some of the darker corners of government.

"Shit." Magda took a large swig of her wine. "There goes everything we've worked for. That bastard is in the pockets of the building development companies. Southwark will become a rich man's playground now he has a say."

O stood and downed her wine, then began to open another bottle of red. "Surely he won't have the power to change things so substantially?" she said.

Jamie sighed. "He has the mandate of being elected on his policies to clean up the streets, so he'll be able to act pretty fast."

"And with Amanda Masters in hospital …" Magda shook her head. "Maybe we should give up, leave London altogether. We can start again somewhere new. I can find a studio somewhere else."

O put down her glass and hugged Magda close, her pale arms stark against Magda's dark clothes.

"Don't say that," O whispered. "If we leave, they will have won. I won't let you go. This is your place, Magda. Your ravens are here, your people are here. Cross Bones needs you." O looked over at Jamie. "Tell her, please."

Jamie took a sip of her wine.

"It certainly seems as if we're being pushed out – arson, violence, evictions, all targeted at one part of the community." She frowned. "But if we go, then this area will be poorer for losing its diversity. You two are figureheads, leaders of the community. Tomorrow, we should start organizing for protest, contact the press and start taking control of the story."

Jamie's voice was stronger than she felt. A few hours ago she had considered leaving herself, and she knew the power that Cameron had on his side. It wouldn't be easy to go up against him.

O stroked Magda's tattooed arm.

"Sleep helps," she said. "Everything looks better in the morning."

Magda nodded and got up slowly, walking into O's bedroom, leaving O and Jamie to make up a bed on the couch.

"Are you sure this is alright?" O asked, patting the pillow.

"It's amazing," Jamie said. "I … don't have many friends."

O leaned forward and kissed her cheek.

"You have us now. Sleep tight."

Jamie lay down and pulled the blankets tight around her. Somehow, despite everything, she felt hope.

***

Jamie woke to the early-morning sun peeking through the curtains. She unfolded herself from O's couch, her body aching from the uncomfortable night, but her mind felt refreshed and clearer now. They could make a plan to mobilize the community and take back what was threatened.

She heard the buzzing of a mobile phone in the next room.

Moments later, the door opened and O stepped out. She wore a plain white t-shirt that ended at the top of her thighs. Her hair was tousled and her face stricken.

"It's Cross Bones," she said. "There are bulldozers on site. They're beginning construction today."

"Bastard," Jamie said. "Cameron must have had this all lined up. And I bet I know which company is involved." She thought of Vera Causa and how much they stood to gain in the area by raising housing prices. That tiny patch of land was worth millions.

Jamie rolled out of bed, quickly pulling on her clothes. Magda emerged from O's room, tucking her black t-shirt into her jeans. Her eyes were puffy as if she'd been crying, but the angles of her face hardened as she made coffee for them all. She texted furiously as the kettle boiled.

"We have a text chain," she explained to Jamie. "Friends of Cross Bones. I'm telling people to get down there ASAP."

Downing their coffee, the three of them headed out into the early morning, through the streets of Southwark down to Cross Bones Graveyard.

***

Jamie could hear the sounds of trucks and heavy machinery as they neared the square and they quickened their pace. Rounding the corner of Redcross Way, the scale of the project was immediately evident. A whole construction team stood waiting at the gates of Cross Bones. There were two bulldozers ready to demolish what was left standing on the derelict ground and diggers idled on standby to begin excavation.

The building site foreman argued with two people who stood in front of the beribboned gates, their arms wrapped around the railings. Jamie recognized one of them – Meg from the Kitchen, her dreadlocks bouncing as she gesticulated at the graveyard.

"You can't come in here," Meg shouted. "This is sacred ground."

"We have the permits," the foreman said. "It's all been cleared by the Mayor. You have to leave or we're calling security to forcibly remove you."

O ran forward to help, Magda following behind.

"Please," O said. "You can't do this."

As O and Magda argued for more time to present their case to the council, Jamie took up a place next to Meg, winding her arms through the gate railings. The metal was cold, and Jamie shivered a little. Clouds gathered overhead, grey skies threatened rain and storms were forecast for later today. Jamie only hoped they would have reached a reprieve by then.

More people from the community arrived. One by one, they stood silently against the railings, backs to the graveyard, hands touching the fence behind them as if part of the structure. Some brought bike chains and padlocks, attaching themselves physically to the barrier.

The air of rebellion was palpable and Jamie found herself thrilled to be a part of it. As a police officer she had only ever been on the other side, viewing protestors as standing in the way of law and order. But now she had a very different perspective. If the graveyard fell to developers, it would be an end to old Southwark. The enrichment of corporations at the expense of the lively, diverse community. But they had this one chance to stop it.

More and more people arrived as O and Magda kept the foreman talking. Soon, the whole length of the side road was lined with people protecting the graveyard, living flesh and blood standing guard over the bones of those who came before.

"Shit," the foreman finally shouted, spinning away from the two women in frustration. He turned to his team. "Bill, get security down here to move this lot on. We have to break ground today. Until then, time out, everyone."

The workmen turned off the vehicle engines and stood in a huddle away from the site, smoking and drinking coffee. A gentle rain began to patter down and the protestors pulled out raincoats and umbrellas, the colorful arcs echoing the multihued ribbons on the gates. Some shared their shelter and soon people were chattering in groups, the tension broken for now. But Jamie watched the foreman on the phone, wary of who he was speaking to. She knew all too well how the upper echelons of power could skirt round regulations.

A couple of guys from a local independent cafe brought down a tray of red velvet cake and took orders for hot drinks. They had elegantly waxed mustaches and wore black and white striped aprons, part of their funky branding. Jamie couldn't help but smile – only in London could protestors get a hand-delivered double shot vanilla latte.

A young man with a guitar began to sing. At first the protestors and workmen watched him with bemused expressions, but as he sang more bawdy songs, they began to laugh. He played tunes that people knew and some protestors began to sing along. Even a couple of the workmen joined in, and for a moment, Jamie wondered if this might be resolved peaceably, that somehow, the community could save this plot.

Then two white vans turned into Redcross Way, parking next to one of the bulldozers.

The doors slid open and five big men emerged from each.

They were all dressed in security uniforms, impeccably dressed, but Jamie didn't think they would mind getting a little messed up. In fact, they looked like they would welcome it. If she had still been in the police, she wouldn't be scared of this lot. There was a hierarchy of authority and the police trumped security, but here, these men held the higher ground and she saw how much they relished it.

The young man stopped playing his guitar and went to stand against the fence, his hands wound protectively around his instrument. Around her, Jamie sensed the unease of the protestors.

She reached for her phone, turning towards the gate, and quickly called the local police station, reporting trouble. Then she texted Missinghall, advising him to get people down here. It was all she could think of to do.

The rain began to fall harder now, spattering the dirt of the graveyard into murky puddles. The foreman stepped towards the gates, a swagger in his step now he had security backup. He held a golf umbrella above his head with the words of the company emblazoned on it.

Vera Causa.

O and Magda walked forward to represent the protestors, ready to go into verbal battle again.

"We have the correct permits," the foreman said, his voice icy calm now. He thrust the appropriate paperwork at them. "You all need to leave immediately so we can start our work. If you don't, you'll be removed by security."

The big men walked down the line of protestors, their eyes fixing on each face, the promise of violence in their posture and clenched fists. They didn't touch anyone but their message was clear.

Jamie watched one tower over an old lady in a moth-eaten fur coat, a remnant of Southwark's past. She lifted her chin at him in defiance and clutched the railings even harder at his sneer. The people of Southwark were indeed a hardy bunch and Jamie wondered where the woman's strength came from.

"We're exercising our right to protest peaceably," O said, her voice strong. Magda stood at her side, her face stony. "You can't use force to remove us. We've called the press and we'll report our story and stop this development."

The foreman shrugged and signaled to the workmen.

Two of them got back into the bulldozers and started the engines, revving them hard. The other workmen began to gather their equipment, ready to move into the graveyard.

The protestors looked at each other, shaking their heads, not knowing what to do.

"Hold still," Magda shouted above the din. "They're trying to intimidate us. They won't touch us."

As the rain hammered down, the security men spread themselves down the line opposite those huddled against the fence. At a signal from their leader, they took a slow, deliberate step forward.

CHAPTER 27

Jamie saw the menace in their eyes, but she didn't believe they would be able to touch the protestors. They were relying on brute intimidation, waiting for the crowd to crack. And it looked like it was beginning to work.

One middle-aged man stepped away from the fence, raising his hands in surrender.

"I'm sorry, O," he called out as he walked away. "I didn't sign up for this."

His defection caused a wave in the group and more began to drop away, heads down against the rain as they retreated. But a core group remained, clustering in front of the main gate, their resolve hardening.

The foreman's phone rang. He answered it and smiled.

He signaled to the head of security and Jamie didn't like what she saw in his eyes. They couldn't touch the protestors – unless someone was protecting them, unless someone would be able to spin this story and stop the police from getting here or preventing charges. It had to be Dale Cameron.

The security men surged forward at the signal and pulled the protestors forcibly from the gates, dragging them kicking and screaming, pushing and shoving hard enough to hurt but not injure too much.

One woman ended up face down in the mud still clutching ribbons from the gate. A security guard stepped on her hand and she screamed. The man smiled and pressed his boot harder.

Jamie moved to help and the man turned to grab her, his meaty fist high. She ducked under and used a knife hand to jab into his throat. He gasped, clutching his neck, his eyes surprised at her retaliation.

Jamie bent to help the woman up, then turned to see two more of the security men walking towards her.

"Feisty little thing, aren't you," one of the men said.

"I'm a former police officer," Jamie snarled at them, standing her ground. "You're all in a lot of trouble for this."

The men laughed. They lunged at the same time and Jamie realized this was no time to fight. There was no way she could come out of this well. Not here, not against these men. She put up her hands and took a step back but the men were already fired up.

They bundled her to the floor, dragging her hands up behind her back, grinding her face into the muddy tarmac.

"Now you stay down," the man whispered, forcing her hands up higher until Jamie felt her shoulders crunch. She let out a whimper and the man relaxed his grip, clearly delighted by her acquiescence.

A roar came from one of the bulldozers. It began to move towards the gates, revving its engine to scare the last protestors out of the way.

It was moving too fast for such a small area, but the man driving was encouraged by the cheers of his co-workers. The rain obscured his vision, hammering down on his windshield as he drove inexorably towards the gates.

Suddenly, Jamie saw O twist out of the grip of one of the security guards and run towards the gates. Magda turned too late to grab her and for a split second, Jamie saw O standing in front of the bulldozer, her body the final obstacle. But the bulldozer didn't stop.

The crunch of metal against gates.

The thud of the vehicle against a body.

Magda's scream.

It all came at once.

The man holding Jamie down released her and she sprang up, running towards the front of the bulldozer. The other workmen were shouting now and the vehicle reversed away. Jamie caught a glimpse of the driver's stricken face. This had all gone too far.

"Call an ambulance," the foreman shouted.

A little group gathered around a fallen figure. O lay against the gate, hands clutched at her belly, eyelids fluttering over a startled gaze. Magda wept by her side, her arms cradling her lover.

"Olivia," she whispered. "Stay with me."

As the rain spattered the ground around them, Jamie heard sirens coming closer. O had stopped the developers today, but at what cost?

***

Jamie leaned her head back against the wall behind her.

Somehow, she had been spared again. In the midst of death and destruction, she walked unharmed. Even though she had begged whatever god there might be to take her instead of her daughter. Even though she had been in the burning caves and near the explosion at the Tate. Did she have some kind of gift like Blake? Or could it be called a curse to watch those you love hurt while you continued to breathe?

Magda sat in silence next to her, staring ahead, her hands clasped so tightly together that her knuckles were white. This waiting was driving them both crazy.

"I'll get us some more coffee," Jamie said. Magda nodded without meeting her eyes.

Jamie walked through the corridors to the hospital coffee shop, navigating by the multicolored department signs. Sterile white walls with the occasional poster encouraging hand sanitation could have been any hospital anywhere. London's complexity disappeared within these walls, individuals reduced to injured body parts.

O lay in surgery with multiple internal injuries from the crush of the bulldozer. The expression on the doctor's face when they had taken her in made Magda weep afresh.

The building work had stopped after the accident, but Jamie knew that it would start again. If not tomorrow, then perhaps the next day or the next. The leaders of the community had been taken out and the rest would now weaken and give up. It was inevitable. The last few days had been about breaking them so they would give up without a fight. Or at least only a pitiful one.

Jamie bought two double shot coffees, some chocolate bars and bananas and headed back to Magda.

"Here you go," Jamie said when she arrived back to find her friend in exactly the same position. "She'll likely be hours yet, so you need to keep your strength up."

"I can't lose her," Magda whispered, turning to Jamie with haunted eyes. "It took me so many years to find someone who accepts all of me."

Jamie took her hand.

"She's not going to die." Jamie put all her hope into her voice, claiming the words as truth as if somehow it would protect O. "She didn't die at the hands of the skin collector, she made it through that and she *will* live now."

Magda nodded. "Yes, you're right. She's a survivor."

"And we have to think positive," Jamie said. "Send her your strength."

Magda took a sip of her coffee.

"The company that wants to develop Cross Bones," she said. "They'll try again, won't they?"

Jamie nodded.

"They have the permits. It's only a matter of time." She paused, thinking of Vera Causa and how entwined they were with the property market in Southwark. Perhaps there was a way. "I do have an inkling of who might be behind it all, though. Perhaps I might be able to find evidence against them. It might help us keep the protest going, get some media attention at least."

"They've taken so much in the last few days, Jamie. If you can find out anything, it might help us keep the community together."

Jamie nodded. She looked at her watch. It was after nine p.m.

"I'll go now. I have a few leads to follow up. Text me or call if you hear anything."

Jamie headed out into the evening, her mind made up.

She had the address of the Vera Causa offices from the research she had done in the last few days. It was time to go to the source and see what she could find.

Getting onto her bike, she rode through the familiar streets, considering what she was about to do. Breaking and entering wasn't new to her – she had broken into a Hoxton studio during the Neville investigation, but Vera Causa was cloaked with secrets. Would she rouse a more powerful force by entering their domain?

She drove along the street where the office was situated. The area was split between residential buildings and new office space. The Vera Causa address was nothing special and there was no sign on the door, no way to know whether this was really the right place. But at least the lights were off.

Jamie parked a little way from the building and then walked back, hands in her pockets. She passed a pub at the head of the street. A couple of smokers stood outside with pints, engrossed in a political argument. The office was at the quieter end, so Jamie walked straight up to the door.

Deliberate action was less obvious than hesitancy. *Confidence inspired confidence*, she thought, echoes of her police training resonating even in this less-than-legal situation.

The door had a numeric keypad, so she wasn't getting in this way without specialist equipment.

Jamie walked around the back of the building. There was a fire escape staircase leading up to the second floor. Stepping lightly, she mounted the stairs, examining the windows and doors on each level as she ascended. They were all locked and alarmed.

She turned to look out over the nearby buildings. The Shard towered above, a beacon of blue light announcing its majestic presence. *It was beautiful*, Jamie thought. *A testament to the power of human creativity and drive. If it can be imagined, it can be created.* That's what she used to tell Polly about the world. *Everything around us first existed as an idea in someone's mind*, she would say. Then they made it happen.

Of course, that was just as true for destruction as for creation. Someone's mind was set against the community of Southwark and Jamie felt a renewed desire to seek them out.

She turned and looked at the upper-level windows. They were all locked. Her eyes scanned upwards onto the roof. There was a skylight built into the tiles and it looked as if it might be open an inch. Jamie glanced down. It was a long way to fall.

She began to climb, pushing herself up with her legs and pulling on the tiles above. *Don't look down, don't look down.* The words a mantra in her mind as she inched her way to the skylight.

It was open a little and she slipped her fingers under, pulling it up slowly. It pivoted and opened with only a tiny creak. It didn't look like it was alarmed.

Jamie turned her body, dropping feet first into an attic space. She stood for a moment, breathing quietly, letting her heart rate return to normal as she listened to the building. It was still, silent, and she sensed it was empty, at least for now. But she didn't want to stay too long.

She clicked on her pen torch.

The attic space was cluttered with piles of boxes. Jamie opened one to find stacked rental agreements from the surrounding area. Another was full of sales receipts from a shop with a local address. With so many boxes and not much time, she couldn't hope to find anything up here.

Jamie walked down the stairs, pausing as one creaked underfoot. Her heart raced, but there was no sound of anyone else here. She continued on.

The first floor had an open-plan office space and a conference room with glass walls. The decor was magnolia and shades of blue, a relaxing professional place. She walked around the desks and checked the computers, but all were password protected or logged off. There were some papers on the desks, all evidence of a real estate management company. Nothing untoward. Jamie's heart sank as she looked around. Clearly Vera Causa was very good at navigating the right side of the law, even if their ethics could be questioned.

At the back of the open-plan area was a separate office area, the size of the space indicating it was for senior management. Jamie pushed open the door and glanced around. It was immaculate, chrome surfaces gleaming. It looked to be entirely paperless, no filing cabinets, no documents left out.

Then she saw something glint in the torchlight. Something that could make all the difference.

CHAPTER 28

IT WAS ONLY A fountain pen, but Jamie recognized it as belonging to Dale Cameron. Its distinctive silver fox-head cap was rare and she remembered him using it to sign paperwork back when she was in the police. It had also been in his top pocket when the news of the Mayoralty was announced. Now, the pen lay on the desk, perpendicular to a clean A4 pad of paper.

With her sleeve over her hand, Jamie picked up the pen, wrapped it in a sheet of paper and put it in her jacket pocket. The pen was useless to her, but perhaps Blake would be able to read something from it that would help.

Jamie walked quickly back up to the attic and climbed out of the skylight, making sure to leave it at the same angle it had been when she'd entered. She slipped down the roof tiles onto the fire escape and then quietly walked away from the office building. The pen seemed to burn in her pocket and she saw Dale Cameron's face in her mind. Like a puppet master, he controlled so much behind the scenes, and she wondered how far his influence stretched. How much further he could go as Mayor.

She roared away on the bike, heading towards Bloomsbury.

***

Blake stood in the kitchen holding an empty tequila bottle. It was the last of the batch and there was no other alcohol in the flat.

Perhaps he would go to the corner store and get a small bottle of vodka. That's all he needed to take the edge off. Or he could go down to Bar-Barian and buy his way into oblivion. In many ways that would be preferable, because right now he didn't know what else to do.

The choice his uncle had offered was a gold chalice laced with poison. He wanted to know about his gift, he wanted to meet his extended family, yet he had seen what they did in the forests of the north in a vision of blood and madness. He should forget the Galdrabók and embrace his life here.

But what life? he thought.

He and Jamie skirted the edges of something but were they both too damaged to take it any further? Without her, there was only casual sex, and with his job under threat, would he even have the choice to stay?

Blake clenched the bottle in his hand, knuckles white. Perhaps he shouldn't fight the addiction anymore. Perhaps it was time to just let it play out. He put the bottle next to the bin, picked up his keys, and grabbed his jacket.

The doorbell rang.

Blake frowned. He wasn't expecting anyone, certainly not this late. He clicked the intercom button.

"Hello," he said.

"It's Jamie." Her voice was soft. Blake's heart leapt in his chest. He put down his jacket and pressed the open button.

"Come up," he said.

Blake pulled open the door, listening to her footsteps climb the stairs, and then she was there, looking up at him from the stairwell. Her dark hair was tied back and there were shadows under her eyes.

"I'm sorry for coming this late," she said.

"It's fine." Blake smiled. "Are you OK?"

Jamie walked up the last few stairs. "It's been a hell of a day, to be honest."

Blake saw the vulnerability in her eyes and pulled her into his arms, hugging her close. She was stiff for a second and then she relaxed, exhaling as she returned his embrace.

She explained what had happened at Cross Bones, about O, the Kitchen, her eviction and the threat to the community.

"That really is a hell of a day," Blake said. "Coffee?"

She stepped away. "Yes please, and then I need your help with something."

He saw the question in her eyes.

"No, I haven't been drinking." He smiled again, this time with an edge of embarrassment. "Although if you'd come ten minutes later, things might have been different."

He wanted to tell her of his uncle's visit, of the possibilities of his gift. But she needed his focus on her now, not on his own dilemma.

Blake put the kettle on and made fresh coffee, carrying the mugs back into the main room. Jamie stood at his window looking out over the rooftops, her eyes fixed on the horizon like she wanted to fly out into the night.

She turned and placed a silver fountain pen wrapped in a piece of paper on his desk.

"I need you to read this," she said. "I don't know what else to do. I'm hoping that you'll see something that could help."

Blake considered his uncle's words, how every time he read strengthened the link between him and his kin. How he opened his mind to the other realm each time and that the *drip drip drip* of darkness would inch into him. He shouldn't do it. But this was for Jamie.

"OK," he said. "But you know I can't promise anything."

She nodded. "Please try anyway."

Blake sat down and took his gloves off. He placed both hands over the pen and lowered his fingertips to the silver, letting the cool metal connect with his skin. He closed his eyes and let the swirling mists rise up in his mind.

He felt an initial resistance, but then he gave into the sensation and dipped through the veil.

The pen was dense with memory, the emotions imprinted upon it holding fast to the metal. Colors swirled about him as Blake began to assume the mantle of the man who owned it. He picked a thread and opened his eyes within the vision.

He looked out at a sea of cameras, of smiling faces, a moment of triumph captured against a backdrop of the City of London. It was the pinnacle of the man's life so far. Blake felt a surge of power, the man's heart pounding as he accepted the position of Mayor. But behind the triumph, there was something darker, a pulse of rotten black that Blake saw as a visible stain. The man gloated over those he looked down upon, for they didn't know his true face.

Blake plucked the darker strings, following them down into a hidden place, closing his eyes again.

He had rarely followed these deeper emotions, preferring to skim on the surface of vision. But this man – Blake's breath caught as he glimpsed a corrupt core under the gleaming surface. The power he wielded was greater than the police, greater than the Mayoralty. He believed he had the power of life and death, who would rise and who would fall in his city. The sense of arousal was strong and as much as he didn't want to, Blake followed that thread.

He opened his eyes within the vision again and saw the chains and hooks of the abattoir above him.

He smelled the metallic hint of blood and machinery.

His hands felt sticky.

Blake looked down through the eyes of the man to see a body that lay on the slab before him, the skinning knife in his hand. A dragon in shades of purple flew across the man's back but there was no life in him left, only his skin would outlast his mortality. The knife hand hovered above the body. For an instant, Blake wanted to pull away in revulsion and drop out of the vision. He stopped himself, controlling the nausea, testing his own limits to stay within.

The man began to cut around the edge of the tattoo, dipping down into the layers of flesh. There was precision in his work and Blake experienced deep concentration and pride. The compartments in the man's mind enabled him to separate his public and private selves. *We all have these two sides,* Blake thought, *but some are more deeply separated than others.* There was no sense that the man saw the body in front of him as a person, only as an artwork in progress. And a way to exercise power against those who cluttered the streets.

But none of this would help Jamie. They needed proof, a way to stop the man.

He let the veil close over the scene and reached lower into the man's emotions. There was a rich vein deeper still in consciousness, a hidden box within the layers the man cloaked his life with. Blake let himself sink into it, and opened his eyes again.

He was in the man's study.

A pair of brown leather wingback chairs sat at oblique angles to a large oak table. Bookshelves lined the walls with an eclectic mix of tomes, from first editions to the latest forensic journals. The man was secure here but there was also a latent excitement, an expectation that went beyond what this room offered.

The man reached for a book on the bookcase and typed in a code, pulling a hidden door open. His arousal was heady and Blake fought to keep himself separate from this man's dark psyche. He understood the temptation to vicariously experience – the visions could allow him that – but like ink into water, it would taint his soul.

The hidden room was a trophy cabinet, Blake could see that immediately. He saw the beaked mask of the Venetian plague doctor, the books of human skin and framed tattoos, skin stretched and pinned into place. The skinning knife, clean and shiny, its blade glittering.

The man opened a safe and pulled out some papers. Blake glimpsed stock certificates with the name Vera Causa on them. The man pushed them aside and reached for a box carved with obscenities. He opened it and pulled out a sheaf of photos. Blake caught sight of a child's face and felt a spike in the man's arousal. He pulled away quickly before the images imprinted themselves on his mind. He had seen enough.

Blake opened his eyes and lifted his hands from the pen. The room swam a little as he refocused on the present, anchoring himself again to the physical world he inhabited. He let his mind scan over his own body, sensing he was back and had separated from the tendrils of the evil he had briefly touched.

Jamie handed him some water silently.

Blake drank several big gulps, letting the cool liquid slide down his throat, latching onto physical sensation. He took a deep breath and turned to face Jamie.

CHAPTER 29

"I THINK THE PEN belongs to the new Mayor, Dale Cameron," Blake said. Jamie didn't look surprised. "OK, you knew that."

Jamie nodded. "But I think he's more than that."

"You're right," Blake said. "I saw the abattoir, the beaked mask from the ball. He has a box full of photos – children – but I pulled away then."

Jamie reached for his hand and squeezed it. "I'm sorry you had to see that," she said. "But now we know."

Blake shook his head. "But it's inadmissible, you know that. The visions mean nothing without physical evidence."

Jamie's eyes glinted in the half light. "I know that, but I have contacts in the police. I can get this to the attention of the right people."

Blake put his head in his hands. The desire for alcohol had subsided, but his head pounded with the aftermath of the visions.

"You need to rest," Jamie said. "I know how much reading takes out of you. Come lie down."

She patted the bed next to her, pulling the covers open for him.

There was a part of Blake that wanted to lean down and kiss her right now, to stroke her bare skin with his scarred hands. Could he read her past? Could he take her pain from her?

But now wasn't the right time. It never seemed to be the right time.

He lay down and closed his eyes. He felt her breath on his cheek and then her lips touched his face in a light kiss. Her weight shifted a little as she leaned down.

"I need to make some calls and then I'll come and rest with you," she whispered. "Sleep now."

Blake wanted to hold onto that moment, he wanted to wait for her to come to bed, but he was exhausted. His mind and body spent. He let go of wanting and slipped into sleep.

***

Jamie heard Blake's breathing change as he fell asleep. His face relaxed and she watched him for a moment. He was a beautiful man and part of her wanted to curl around him and kiss his caramel skin, taste his body. He would wake in the night and they would finally take things further. All she had to do was slip into bed next to him.

But his vision had shaken her and Jamie knew she wouldn't sleep now.

Dale Cameron had been her boss in the police, but she had glimpsed his darker side several times. She had tried to ignore her suspicions before, but now she was sure that it must have been him in the smoke of the Hellfire Caves, covering up the scandal for his aristocratic friends. He procured the victims for the RAIN agency and now he was cleaning up the city in a much more personal way.

Jamie picked up her motorcycle helmet and gloves. She looked down at Blake's sleeping face once more, fixing his image in her mind.

This wasn't his responsibility. She had to do this alone.

She picked up the pen and put it in her pocket. Then she slipped out of the flat, mounted her bike and roared back towards Southwark.

The Mayor's new office was in the Shard, the tallest building in Europe, a tower of glass that rose above the ancient city like an angel's spear pointing the way to Heaven. Jamie parked below it and looked up. It was beautiful, a fitting place for Dale Cameron to survey his new domain. Jamie thought of the temptation of Jesus in the desert when the Devil had taken him to a high place and offered him the world if only he would call on the angels to lift him up. It seemed as if Cameron had already taken his deal with the Devil.

It was late, but she knew Cameron's habits from the police. He often worked late into the night, and in the first few days of his Mayoralty it was likely that he was still at the office. She also still had his mobile number.

She stood at the main entrance, closed and locked for the night. Jamie dialed Cameron's number.

It rang once, twice, three times. Her heart sank as she realized that she might not have the reckoning she craved tonight.

"Jamie Brooke." Cameron's voice was calm and assured. "I'm a little surprised to hear from you, especially at this late hour."

"I'd like to talk to you," Jamie said, her heart pounding. She didn't really have a plan as such, but her anger had carried her this far. She had to see it through now. "I remember how you used to work this late in the police." She paused. "I miss those times."

There was a moment of silence and she wondered if she had laid it on too thick.

A click and a whirr and the door slid open.

"Come up. Take the right-hand lift."

DEVIANCE

Jamie walked in, her footsteps echoing on the marble slabs underfoot. This place oozed wealth and power. No wonder Cameron liked it here.

The lift made her feel slightly queasy as it zoomed upwards. She took her phone out and activated the recording app, slipping it back into her pocket as the doors pinged. Jamie stepped out to find Cameron standing at the doorway to his office, a bottle of burgundy in his hand. He wore a grey suit that looked like it cost more than Jamie's motorbike. He was clean shaven and she could smell a hint of cologne. Enough to woo the senses, not overpower them.

"Drink?" he said, holding up the bottle. The movement revealed a Patek Philippe watch on his wrist. "I was about to have one myself and after all, it's not something we ever did when we worked together."

Jamie nodded. "That would be great."

He turned and she followed him through the open-plan workspace into his office. There were piles of boxes everywhere, paperwork strewn over desktops and pictures still in bubble wrap.

"We're still moving in," Cameron said, pouring the wine into two Riedel glasses. His eyes twinkled with excitement. "Lots to do. Exciting times for the city."

Jamie felt the edge of his charisma as she sipped the wine. He had the ability to make people feel special, his gaze a sunbeam of energy, like they were the only person in the world to him.

"It's good to see you, Jamie," Cameron said softly. "You were a great Detective, and I'm sorry you left when you did. I apologize if I made things hard for you, especially when you were coping with the death of your daughter."

Jamie let him talk. He was still a smooth bastard, that was for sure. No wonder the city loved him. But now she knew what was underneath that facade and she just had to draw it out.

"I need people I can trust now and as Mayor, I can make connections for you," Cameron continued, his voice confident. "You could come and work for me. Or you could go back into the police if you want, perhaps even at a higher level. I can make that happen. Or I know some people in private security, where you could earn more money than you ever have before, doing the work you love."

She pulled the silver pen from her pocket.

"I actually came to return this," she said, laying it on the desk.

His grey eyes narrowed a little as he reached for it.

"I wondered where that had gone." He looked at her closely. "Where did you find it?"

"I've been doing some private investigation work on behalf of the Southwark community since the murders. We've had difficult times in recent days."

"I'm sorry to hear that," Cameron said, his response almost automated, trotted out in interviews to display compassion. But the words were empty, his eyes suspicious.

"The company behind the evictions and the security company at Cross Bones is called Vera Causa. I found your pen at their offices."

Cameron raised an eyebrow. "I've been doing a lot of community work for the Mayoral campaign. I must have left it there. Thanks for returning it." He paused for a moment, leaning back in his chair. The shadows shifted and for a moment, he was shrouded in darkness.

He pointed to a staircase in the corner of the room. "Let's go up to the roof. There's something I want to show you. Something I think you'll appreciate with your love for the city."

He pushed his chair out and walked up the stairs without looking back.

Jamie sat for a moment. Cameron was dangerous and following him was a risk, but she needed evidence to stop him. She grabbed the silver pen from his desk and slipped it back in her pocket before following him up the stairs.

CHAPTER 30

BLAKE WOKE IN THE darkness of his room. His heart pounded as he emerged from a nightmare of gleaming knives and blood.

Jamie.

She had been here when he had fallen asleep and now she was gone. A coldness swept over him as he realized that she must have gone to meet Cameron. After his reading last night, she had decided to face him alone.

Blake jumped out of bed and grabbed his phone, dialing Jamie's number quickly. It rang and rang and then switched to voicemail.

"Damn it, Jamie," he whispered. He needed to get down there, but he needed local help.

"Magda, it's Blake Daniel. We met at O's flat earlier this week. I'm sorry to call so late."

"Oh, not at all." Magda's voice was dull. "I'm back at the hospital and O is recovering from surgery. Maybe Jamie told you?"

"Yes," Blake said. "It's about Jamie. I need your help."

He explained about his reading, his suspicions that Jamie had gone to meet Cameron.

"I'm coming," Magda said, her voice stronger now, galvanized into action. "This has gone too far. I will not have another of our number hurt tonight. I'll meet you on the corner of Stoney Street next to Borough Market."

***

Jamie emerged from the stairwell onto one of the very top floors of the Shard. The view was stunning, a 360-degree panorama of London with the river a dark ribbon running through its heart. This level was still under construction with glass panels enclosing three sides of the structure, but the east side and the roof were partially open to the elements, with only a safety barrier blocking access.

A gust of wind whipped through and Jamie pulled her jacket close about her shoulders. The metal girders creaked a little and the glass rattled, the sound of the building shifting in the sky.

Cameron stood looking north over the city, his nose inches from the glass. He turned at Jamie's approach.

"Isn't it amazing up here?" His grey eyes shone with passion. "This is where I come to get some perspective, and I hope that you will be able to see as I do." Jamie stepped slowly towards him, needing to get closer to record his words. He pointed out, sweeping his arm in a wide arc. "This is London, as far as you can see. The city is not just Southwark, it's not just your Kitchen or Cross Bones Graveyard. It's millions of people who deserve a city where they can thrive. A city that has been cleaned of those who don't deserve to be here. Like a cancer, they must be cut out so the healthy body can survive."

Jamie looked down into the streets of Southwark. She thought she could see Cross Bones Graveyard below them, a patch of dark in the bright orange spectrum of streetlights.

How insignificant our lives are, Jamie thought. The Shard was built upon the ground of an ancient borough and the blood of two millennia had been spilled here. Now the anger of the Outcast Dead rose up, the shades of those buried by the advance of the rich and powerful over the years.

She placed a hand on the glass.

"I don't see the city as you do," she said softly. "I see people who need help, communities that need leaders who will stand up to your plans." She turned. "Like we did at Cross Bones."

"And look how that ended for your friends," Cameron spat as he walked behind her and stood at the top of the stairs.

"I *will* clean up London, Jamie," he said, his eyes cold, a steel grey as hard as the girders that surrounded them. "I have powerful backers who have the money and power we need for rejuvenation and redevelopment."

"But you'll destroy the diversity that makes this borough a unique historical community," Jamie said.

"Local color is overrated." Cameron chuckled. "People would rather have more wealth. They've demonstrated that in the way they voted and it's time your 'community' moved on. I'm only helping them move on faster."

Cameron cocked his head to one side, regarding her as if she were a problem to be solved. Jamie tensed, realizing how much of a mistake she had made in coming up here.

She darted sideways, ducking under his arm as she rushed for the stairs.

He caught her arm, swinging her back around. Her phone fell out of her pocket, the case smashing on the concrete floor as it spun towards the open edge of the building.

She struggled against him, bringing her arms up fast to break his hold. But he was quick and strong, punching her in the solar plexus sharply with a broad fist.

Jamie dropped to her knees, winded and gasping for breath.

"You should have died that night in the Hellfire Caves,"

Cameron hissed as he grabbed her hair. "You should have burned alongside your daughter's body."

He dragged her over to the open east side as she struggled against him. Cameron kicked her phone out, sending it spinning into the void.

"You won't be needing that anymore."

In the split second he watched it fall, Jamie grabbed his fist with both hands, forcing her thumbs into the pressure points and twisted hard.

Cameron grunted, releasing his grip for a second. Jamie turned away on her knees, scrambling for the exit, trying to get up.

His boot crunched down on her ankle and strong hands grabbed the back of her jeans, tugging her towards the opening.

"You're only leaving one way," he said, yanking Jamie over and then kicking her in the stomach, his face contorted in a snarl.

She curled inwards, trying to protect herself, pain shooting through her. Her fingers scrabbled for the pen in her pocket, clutching it in one fist.

As he kicked again, Jamie grabbed for his foot and pulled it towards her, tugging him off balance. She scrambled on top of him, using the pen to stab him in the groin. Once. Twice. He howled in pain and doubled over.

She took her chance. Jamie got up and ran for the exit.

A crackle behind her.

A burning pain in her back.

The shuddering agony of electricity shot through her and she crumpled to the floor, limbs jerking. Jamie's mind was screaming even as her body was frozen by the shock.

Cameron stood over her, the police-issue Taser in one hand.

"It's been so hard for you lately, hasn't it?" He straightened his tie then bent to her feet. "First you lose your daughter, then your job, then you're evicted. Your community is crumbling around you. It's no wonder you had to end it all. But at least you chose to jump from somewhere with a great view."

He picked up Jamie's feet and dragged her paralyzed body across the floor towards the east opening.

CHAPTER 31

JAMIE COUNTED IN HER mind, knowing that the complete paralysis only lasted a few seconds. She could start to feel a tingle in her limbs again but she remained still, only hoping that she would get her strength back in time.

Cameron dropped her feet and swept aside the safety barrier. The wind was stronger now, buffeting them as he dragged her closer to the edge.

"Bracing, isn't it?" He grinned, and Jamie saw a mania born of addiction to power there. Cameron was used to getting everything he wanted, destroying lives in the shadows while he stood squeaky clean in public. He bent to pick up her feet again.

Jamie felt tingling in her arms and legs. *One more second*, she thought. *Don't move too soon.* The gaping hole in the building was only a meter away now and she struggled to relax as Cameron dragged her closer.

Then she saw it.

A blowtorch ready for the next day's welding. It was within reach, but she only had one chance.

"I'll make sure the papers write something good about your death," Cameron said. "Perhaps I'll even do the eulogy at your funeral." He turned and smiled. "Fitting, don't you think?"

Jamie lunged for the blowtorch as she kicked out with both feet.

Cameron fell backwards, teetering on the edge. He grabbed for the side girder, pulling himself back in.

Jamie pressed the switch on the blowtorch, sending a spurt of flame into his face.

Cameron screamed in rage and pain, protecting his face with his hands. The smell of singed hair and burned flesh filled the air. He charged her, bellowing his anger, blocking her path to the exit as he ran at her like a bull.

Jamie dropped the torch, ducked away. She just needed to stay out of his reach.

Thick metal girders led up to the next level. Jamie ran for them and began to climb, fixing her eyes on the rivets in front of her, trying to ignore the sheer drop beneath, one thousand feet to the ground below.

"Come back here, bitch." Cameron's voice was rough and he breathed heavily as he pulled himself after her.

Hand over hand, Jamie climbed. She reached the next level only to find the floor hadn't been finished and there was no way to get down again. She could only go up.

The Shard tapered as it rose into the night sky, the girders getting thinner the higher she climbed. Jamie could hear Cameron's breathing below her. Her arms shook with effort as she pulled herself up another inch.

***

Blake arrived at Borough Market to find Magda gazing up at the Shard through binoculars.

"The Mayor's new office is up there," she said, focusing the lenses on the upper levels. "If Jamie's up there, we might be able to see her."

Blake stood, his fists clenched as Magda slowly scanned

the building. Every part of him wanted to be with Jamie now. He'd been crazy to sleep after telling her about Cameron. He should have known she would take action.

"Oh no." Magda's voice chilled Blake with its dark intensity.

"What is it?" he said, grabbing the binoculars from her and training them on the upper levels.

"Look at the east corner," Magda said. "That must be her."

Blake could make out a lone figure clambering up one of the exposed metal girders on the open east side of the building.

Behind her, another figure climbed with strong movements, gaining on her quickly.

"Jamie…" Blake whispered. "Hold on." He spun to Magda. "How do we get up there?"

She shook her head. "There are so many levels of security. We won't get in that way." Her eyes narrowed. "But there might be something."

"Anything," Blake said. "Please. We have to help her."

"You have your gift," Magda said. "I have my own."

She pulled one of her sleeves up, revealing the tattooed ravens that whirled on her arm. Pulling a small penknife from her bag, she cut a symbol into the feathers of one of the birds, tracing three whorls into her skin. A bead of blood welled and dripped down her arm to the ground.

As it splashed on the earth, Magda began to whistle.

The tune was soft at first and then stronger, the notes a Celtic refrain of growing power.

The wind changed and the cold made Blake shiver as Magda called on the Morrigan, the shape-shifting goddess of war, fate and death. She who roamed the battlefields in the shape of a raven, choosing those who would live and who would die.

As Magda whistled into the wind, her hands held high, Blake heard the beat of wings on the air. A flock of ravens appeared out of the night and flew overheard, wheeling about her. They were strangely silent, their beady eyes looking down on the one who called them.

Magda turned towards the Shard and her whistling song switched to a harsher refrain.

She pointed at the top of the spire and the birds streamed away from her, cawing loudly now, a jarring cacophony that drowned out the sound of the city.

They flew up and soon a dark cloud obscured the top of the Shard. Blake could only pray for the outcome above.

CHAPTER 32

JAMIE'S ARMS BURNED AS she tried to haul herself up a little further, inching away from Cameron into the highest reaches of the building. The wind buffeted her and she clung to the metal, heart pounding as she hung above the void, vertigo making her head spin.

She looked down to see him inches below her foot, his hand stretched out to grab her.

"I will see you fall tonight," Cameron said. "So give in to it, Jamie. Lean out and you will see your daughter again."

Jamie stamped down on his grasping fingers.

"Polly never gave up," she said, panting with the effort of holding on and trying to kick him away. "Neither will I."

Cameron grabbed her foot and twisted it. Jamie gasped in pain as he forced her leg sideways off the side of the girder. Off balance for a second, she grabbed for another hold and slipped down a few inches.

Cameron reached for her and Jamie saw her death in his eyes.

As his hand stretched out, a stream of ravens swirled up in a vortex into his face, beaks and claws ripping at his skin.

Cameron screamed, his arms waving at them, trying to beat them off even as they pecked and shredded his flesh.

Jamie put her hands over her face, clinging to the girder

as the birds dive-bombed Cameron, bodies repeatedly thunking against his. Individually the ravens were nothing, but together, they forced him from the girder inch by inch.

Two birds landed on his hair, claws ripping it away in bloody chunks. He raised both his hands, losing his grip, and for a moment he teetered on the edge of the girder.

The flock wheeled, and together they pounded into him.

Dale Cameron plummeted off the Shard, his dying scream drowned out by the triumphant cawing of the ravens.

***

Jamie couldn't move.

She clung to the girder, eyes closed, as the wind whipped about her. The birds were gone, Cameron was gone, but she was still at the top of the building, hanging above certain death. Her strength was fading, her limbs ached, and she only wanted to close her eyes and let it all go.

Climbing down seemed like an overwhelming impossibility – but perhaps she didn't have to. With Cameron gone, the circle could be closed on the cases she'd been involved with. She could be with Polly if she just relaxed. The end would be swift, she knew that.

But then Polly's voice came to her in the wind. *Dance for me, Mum.*

Jamie held on. *One more minute*, she thought.

***

It seemed like a long time later when she heard a voice calling her name.

"Jamie," the voice called softly. Blake's voice. "It's OK. You can come back now. It's safe. Please, Jamie. Look at me."

He was here.

Jamie opened her eyes and looked down through the girders to the platform below. Blake stood there, his hands outstretched towards her. Behind him, Magda stood like a dark guardian angel.

"Inch back down towards me," Blake said. "Just a little way and then I can reach for you."

Blake's voice was soft, but in his tone she heard a promise. "Please, Jamie."

Slowly, she stretched out a leg, her muscles shaking as she gripped the metal with all her strength, easing backwards down the girder.

She inched her way down as her friends called encouragement, every step a huge effort.

Finally, she felt Blake's hand on her foot.

"I'm here," he said. "A little closer and then I'll help you in."

She pushed herself with every last bit of energy she could summon. Then his arms were pulling her into the safety of the tower, into his embrace.

CHAPTER 33: A WEEK LATER

A TRAIN RATTLED ALONG the tracks high on the overbridge, the rhythmic sound a back note to the folk band playing below in Cross Bones Graveyard. Jamie strolled through the open gates, still hung with ribbons commemorating the dead but today flung wide to welcome the community. Towering above her, the Shard rose into a blue sky, its glass panels reflecting the sun like a beacon for the city.

Families walked around the flowerbeds and Jamie watched as one little girl bent to smell a pink rose, her little face lighting up with pleasure as the petals stuck to her nose. Jamie smiled. *Polly would have loved it here*, she thought, but the pang of grief for her daughter was more a dull ache than a sharp pain now. It was settling, she realized. This community and the purpose she had found here gave her something to live for.

Applause rang out across the green as the band finished one song and then launched into a reel. The dancing began again, bare feet pounding the ground where the dead lay beneath. Jamie thought that the women and children who rested under this earth would relish the celebration. Perhaps they had danced here long ago, a moment of pleasure that connected across the generations.

Magda and O spun together in the crowd, laughing as

they danced. O wore a flowery summer dress that floated around her and Magda was her dark opposite in customary tight black jeans and t-shirt. Jamie looked around and realized that she knew many of the people there. This was her community too now.

O spotted Jamie and walked over, her blonde hair shining in the sun. She grabbed Jamie's hands and spun her around to the tune.

"Isn't this wonderful?" O said with a delighted laugh. "Everyone has come out to celebrate. Finally, Cross Bones can be an official memorial garden."

The last few days had been crazy. Dale Cameron's death had officially been ruled a suicide after the contents of his locked room had been leaked to the press. His part in the Southwark murders was still being established, but Jamie had heard from Missinghall that there was evidence from years of criminal activity to go through and the scandal had rocked the upper echelons of power.

The new Mayor, Amanda Masters, had opened her first week by giving Cross Bones Graveyard to the people of Southwark and providing new funding to the Kitchen. The community rallied, and together they were making this a sanctuary for those outcast in life as well as death. Magda and O were leading the development team and Jamie would join them in the next week. It was time she used her skills to build and nurture instead of clean up the aftermath of violence. It felt good to be part of something new, something vibrant.

Magda walked up and kissed Jamie on the cheek, her smile wide as she surveyed the happy crowd.

"Thank you for coming, Jamie. We really couldn't have done this without you." She put her arms around O, pulling her tight against her body. O giggled and nuzzled against her. "And I might have lost Olivia without you."

"Get a room," Jamie laughed, pushing them away, and they skipped back to the reel.

"Fancy a dance?" The voice caught her by surprise and she turned quickly.

Blake stood there, holding a bunch of purple tulips. He ran a gloved hand nervously over his buzzcut.

"I ... I hope it's OK that I came. I brought flowers for the memorial."

"They're gorgeous," Jamie said.

She reached out and touched his arm, her fingers caressing his caramel skin before linking her arm with his. He smelled of pine forests after rain.

"I thought you were going north for a trip," Jamie said. "Did you change your mind?"

"That can wait," Blake said, his voice soft. "I have more important things to focus on here."

Jamie looked up and met his eyes. She saw a promise there, something they could build upon, a new beginning.

"We can lay the flowers together," she said.

ENJOYED DEVIANCE?

Thanks for joining Jamie and Blake in *Deviance*. If you enjoyed the book, a review would be much appreciated as it helps other readers discover the story.

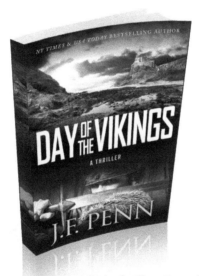

Get a free copy of the bestselling thriller, *Day of the Vikings*, an ARKANE thriller featuring Blake Daniel, when you sign up to join my Reader's Group. You'll also be notified of giveaways, new releases and receive personal updates from behind the scenes of my books.

Click here to get started:

www.JFPenn.com/free

AUTHOR'S NOTE

As with all my books, this one is based on real places and then spun off into a new direction for the story. For images relating to the book, check out the Deviance board on Pinterest: www.pinterest.com/jfpenn/deviance/

Cross Bones Graveyard

Cross Bones is a post-medieval burial ground, that much is true, since excavations found an overcrowded graveyard during the construction of the London Underground Jubilee Line.

John Constable, a Southwark writer, is responsible for the interpretation of it as an unconsecrated graveyard for the Outcast Dead, women who were licensed by the church to work as prostitutes and their children, their sin used to fund the lifestyle and buildings of the clergy. John is an urban shaman under the name John Crow, who also channeled a Winchester Goose to write *The Southwark Mysteries*. He also leads walks around the borough. You can find more about his work here at www.SouthwarkMysteries.co.uk

The character of Magda Raven was influenced by John Constable/John Crow, and also by the book *Pastrix* by Nadia Bolz-Weber.

When I first started writing the book, Cross Bones Grave-yard was under the threat of development by Transport for London, but in Jan 2015, Bankside Open Spaces Trust was given temporary planning permission and a three-year lease for a memorial garden.

You can find videos and more information at www.crossbones.org.uk

Tattoos

If you want to know more about the meaning of tattoos and body modification, then check out *Pagan Fleshworks: The Alchemy of Body Modification* by Maureen Mercury.

You can see tattoos I love on the Pinterest board and yes, I am intending to get ink!

Octopus

The scene that Blake reads in O's pendant is from my own scuba diving experience at the Poor Knights Islands in New Zealand years ago. A huge octopus swam by, stopping for a moment to hang in the water and check me out before swimming on. I've seen a lot of octopi in holes and crevices but this is the only one I've seen in open water. I had the sense of something so alien, yet also intelligent. I've seen the same look in the eyes of dolphins when swimming wild with them.

This fascination with octopi led to the emergence of O's tattoo in *Desecration*, so I wanted to write about its origin story here.

Sex trade in London

It's fascinating how much of London is shaped by the history of the sex trade. The main books used for my research were *City of Sin* by Catharine Arnold and *The Secret History of Georgian London: How the Wages of Sin Shaped the Capital* by Dan Cruickshank

MORE BOOKS BY J.F.PENN

Thanks for joining Jamie and Blake in *Deviance*.

Sign up at www.JFPenn.com/free to be
notified of the next book in the series and
receive my monthly updates and giveaways.

* * *

Brooke and Daniel Psychological Thrillers

Desecration #1
Delirium #2
Deviance #3

* * *

Mapwalker Dark Fantasy Thrillers

Map of Shadows #1
Map of Plagues #2
Map of the Impossible #3

If you enjoy **Action Adventure Thrillers**, check out the
ARKANE series as Morgan Sierra and Jake Timber solve
supernatural mysteries around the world.

Stone of Fire #1
Crypt of Bone #2
Ark of Blood #3
One Day In Budapest #4

Day of the Vikings #5
Gates of Hell #6
One Day in New York #7
Destroyer of Worlds #8
End of Days #9
Valley of Dry Bones #10
Tree of Life #11

* * *

For more **dark fantasy,** check out:

Risen Gods
The Dark Queen
A Thousand Fiendish Angels:
Short stories based on Dante's Inferno

More books coming soon.

You can sign up to be notified of new releases, giveaways
and pre-release specials - plus, get a free book!

www.JFPenn.com/free

If you loved the book and have a moment to spare, I would
really appreciate a short review on the page where you
bought the book. Your help in spreading the word is grate-
fully appreciated and reviews make a huge difference to
helping new readers find the series.

Thank you!

ABOUT J.F.PENN

J.F.Penn is the Award-nominated, New York Times and USA Today bestselling author of the ARKANE action adventure thrillers, Brooke & Daniel Psychological Thrillers, and the Mapwalker fantasy adventure series, as well as other stand-alone stories.

Her books weave together ancient artifacts, relics of power, international locations and adventure with an edge of the supernatural. Joanna lives in Bath, England and enjoys a nice G&T.

You can follow Joanna's travels on Instagram
@jfpennauthor and also on her podcast at
BooksAndTravel.page.

* * *

Sign up for your free thriller,
Day of the Vikings, and updates from behind
the scenes, research, and giveaways at:

www.jfpenn.com/free

* * *

Connect with Joanna:
www.JFPenn.com
joanna@JFPenn.com
www.Facebook.com/JFPennAuthor
www.Instagram.com/JFPennAuthor

* * *

For writers:

Joanna's site, www.TheCreativePenn.com, helps people write, publish and market their books through articles, audio, video and online courses.

She writes non-fiction for authors under Joanna Penn and has an award-nominated podcast for writers, The Creative Penn Podcast.

ACKNOWLEDGEMENTS

For Jonathan. Thank you for joining me on sex tours of Southwark and indulging my weird obsessions at the Tattoo Convention.

Thanks to Jen Blood, my fantastic editor, to Wendy Janes for proofreading and thanks to Jane Dixon-Smith for cover design and interior print formatting.

Lightning Source UK Ltd.
Milton Keynes UK
UKHW010056100223
416720UK00001B/331